A Garland Series

The English Stage
Attack and Defense 1577 - 1730

A collection of 90 important works
reprinted in photo-facsimile in 50 volumes

edited by
Arthur Freeman
Boston University

The Schoole of Abuse

by

Stephen Gosson

A Reply to Gosson's
Schoole of Abuse

by

Thomas Lodge

with prefaces
for the Garland Edition by

Arthur Freeman

Garland Publishing, Inc., New York & London

1973

Library of Congress Cataloging in Publication Data

Gosson, Stephen, 1554-1624.
   The schoole of abuse.

   (The English stage: attack and defense, 1577-
1730)
    Reprint of the 1579 editions.
    1. Theater--Moral and religious aspects.
2. Gosson, Stephen, 1554-1624. The schoole of
abuse. I. Lodge, Thomas, 1558?-1625. A rely to
Stephen Gosson's Schoole of abuse. II. Title.
III. Series.
PR2279.G6S4 1973   828'.3'07   76-170402
ISBN 0-8240-0585-6

The Schoole of Abuse

Stephen Gosson

Preface

One of the most celebrated of all attacks on the stage, Gosson's Schoole of Abuse *(1579) is also bibliographically one of the most complex. Gosson's matter has been discussed in detail by Collier, Chambers, Ringler, Arthur Kinney (*SEL *VII), and by commentators on Sidney, but his text has yet to be correctly established or even described. Pending the appearance of a full critical edition, such as that prepared by Professor Kinney, some more plausible reprint than Collier's or Arber's is necessary, and some discussion of the circumstances of printing no less so.*

The Schoole of Abuse *was entered to Thomas Woodcocke on 22 July 1579. Eleven copies are now known to exist, apparently all in some manner different. The most obvious distinction, and that by which the new* STC *will divide* STC *12097 from 12097.5, is the spelling on the title page of "Schoole": the former number will designate those which read "Shoole" instead — as in the Huntington title we reprint in our appendix; the latter* *those which correctly read "Schoole." But beyond this simple difference, every sheet is known in two alternative settings with concomitant variants, and the assembly by quires of each copy varies, apparently indiscriminately, as well. To explain this anomaly William Ringler (*Stephen Gosson *[Princeton, N.J., 1942], esp. pp. 26-8 and 140-04) suggested a "double printing," i.e., one of three thousand copies, perhaps commissioned by the London city fathers (as was Anthony Munday's* Blast of Retrait, *1580). Professor Kinney, however, has preferred to distinguish two "editions," i.e., ideal or consistent settings, to which one may possibly object that no copy extant represents either ideal in its entirety.* STC *(1926) observed no "edition" distinction, and the late William A. Jackson cites in his* STC MS *working memoranda the earlier Houghton Library card, distinguishing between three groups of variants which "may refer to state rather than issue, and . . . may occur in other combinations than those [i.e., three "issues"] here mentioned." New* STC, *as mentioned above, will discriminate simply by title, noting that copies of each have quires in mixed assembly. We have chosen, therefore, to reprint a specific copy (British Museum 1076. a. 6) with*

PREFACE

defects made up from another (Huntington 61175), and the "Shoole" title page as well from the latter; but a fully edited text with all variants is still much a desideratum.

The collation is similarly curious. The first gathering in seven of the then nine known copies examined by Ringler "lacked" *1 and *8 (i.e. [Hand] 1 and 8) of the first octavo sheet; in fact they all collate χ1, [Hand] 3-4, ² χ1. Subsequently the collation runs simply A-E⁸ F⁵ (Ringler has it F⁶, with F6 "lacking" in all copies); F5ʳ being simply Woodcocke's device (McKerrow 247), the verso blank. One might suppose that F were in fact a half-sheet, and F5, missing in most copies, a fold-over from the preliminary quire. Thus [Hand] 1 or 8 would be accounted for, and the collation rendered a little more plausible; but I am offering an hypothesis only.

In 1942 Ringler knew of nine copies, viz., British Museum 1076. a. 6 (lacks F4-5), Bodley-Linc., lacking E6-F5, Bodley-Malone, lacking F5, Cambridge University (lacking F5), Rosenbach Company (lacking E6-F5, D4 in facsimile), Huntington 61175 and 61176 (lacks B2 and F5), Emmanuel College Cambridge (not seen) and Folger (not seen). To these we may now add copies

9

PREFACE

at Rylands and in the collection of Mr. Wilmarth Lewis (the Horace Walpole-Britwell copy), and note that the Rosenbach Company example (in fact W.A. White's, bought in 1910, but not in the 1926 Handlist) passed to Harvard in 1941. As above, we have chosen to reprint British Museum 1076. a. 6, with F4-5 supplied from Huntington 61175.

The Schoole of Abuse *was reprinted in 1587 (STC 12098), and three unsatisfactory modern reprint editions (Somers Tracts, Shakespeare Society [ed. J.P. Collier], and Arber) have appeared. A curious seventeenth-century echo of the text has been preserved in manuscript: entitled "The Schoole of Wickednesse Or a Satir against Poets Players and other Caterpillers of the Nation By: S: G:," it is evidently an attempt to pass off* verbatim *the old text as new, to a new patron ("the Hon[oura]ble C: B: Esq," rather than Sir Philip Sidney), in the practice of which spelling and punctuation are modernized, and the strictly contemporary allusions to specific plays and playhouses eliminated. From the collection of Sir Thomas Phillipps, it was lot 1508 at Sotheby's, 14 June 1971. Sotheby's date it [c. 1680]; I should myself think it somewhat earlier.*

PREFACE

STC *12097, 12097.5; Lowe-Arnott-Robinson 246-7.*

May, 1972   A. F.

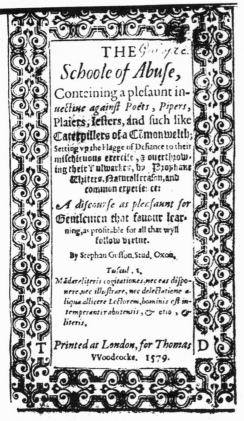

THE *Gosson*

Schoole of Abuse,

Conteining a plesaunt in-
uectiue against *Poëts, Pipers,*
Plaiers, Iesters, and such like
Caterpillers of a Comonwelth;
Setting vp the Flagge of Defiance to their
mischieuous exercise, & ouerthrow-
ing their Bulwarkes, by Prophane
Writers, Naturall reason, and
common experie: ce:

A discourse as pleasaunt for
Gentlemen that fauour learning, as profitable for all that wyll
follow vertue.

By Stephan Gosson. Stud. Oxon.

Tuscul . 1.

Mã dare literis cogitationes, nec eas dispo-
nere, nec illustrare, nec delectatione a-
liqua allicere Lectorem, hominis est in-
temperanter abutentis, & otio, &
literis.

Printed at London, for *Thomas*
VVoodcocke. 1579.

G. STEEVENS.

¶ To the right noble
Gentlemã, Master Philip Sidney
Esquier, Stephan Gosson wisheth health
of body, wealth of minde, rewarde
of vertue, aduauncement of honour,
and good successe in godly
affaires.

Aligula lying in
Fraunce with a
greate armie of
fighting menne,
brought all his
force, on a sudden
to the Sea side, as though hee in-
tended to cutte ouer, and inuade
Englande: when he came to the
shore, his Souldiers were presently set in araye, him selfe shipped
in a small barke, weyed Ancors,
and lanched out; he had not played long in the Sea, vvasting too

☞ 3   and

and fro, at his pleasure, but he returned agayne, stroke sayle, gaue allarme to his souldiers in token of battaile, & charged euerie man too gather cockles. I knowe not (right worshipfull) whether my selfe be as frantike as Caligula in my proceedings, becaufe that after I haue set out the flag of defiance to some abuses, I may seeme well ynough too strike vp the drumme, and bring all my power to a vaine skirmishe. The title of my book doth promise much, the volume you see is very little: & sithens I can not beare out my follie by authoritie, like an Emperour, I wil craue pardon for my Phrenzie, by submission, as your woorshippes too commaunde. The Schoole which

I builde

I builde, is narrowe, and at the firste blushe appeareth but a doggehole; yet small Cloudes carie water; slender threedes sowe sure stitches; little heares haue their shadowes; blunt stones whette kniues; from hard rockes, flowe soft springes; the whole worlde is drawen in a mappe; Homers Iliades in a nutte shell; a Kings picture in a pennie; Little Chestes may holde greate Treasure; a fewe Cyphers contayne the substáce of a rich Merchant; The shortest Pamphlette maye shrowde matter; The hardest heade may giue light; and the harshest penne maye sette downe somewhat woorth the reading.

Hee that hath bin shooke with

a fierce ague, giueth good counsell to his friends when he is wel: When Ouid had roated long on the Seas of wantonnesse, hee became a good Pilot to all that followed, and printed a carde of euerie daunger: and I perswade my selfe, that seeing the abuses which I reueale, trying thē thorowly to my hurt, and bearing the stench of thē yet in my owne nose; I may best make the frame, found the schoole, and reade the first lecture of all my selfe, too warne euery man to auoyde the perill. Wherein I am contrary to Simonides, for hee was euer slowe to vtter, and swift to conceale, beeing more sorrowefull, that he had spoken, then that hee had held his peace, But I accuse

my

my selfe of difcourtefie too my
friendes, in keeping thefe abufes
fo long fecret, and nowe thinke
my duetie difcharged in layinge
them open.

A good Phifition when the
difeafe cannot bee cured within,
thrufteth the corruption out in
the face, and deliuereth his Patient to the Chirurgion: Though
my skill in Phificke bee fmall, I
haue fome experience in thefe
maladyes, which I thruft out
with my penne too euery mans
viewe, yeelding the ranke flefhe
to the Chirurgions knife, and fo
ridde my handes of the cure, for
it paffeth my cunning too heale
them priuily.

If your Worfhippe vouch-
fafe to enter the Schoole doore,
and

and walke an hower or twaine
within for your pleafure, you
fhall fee what I teach, which
prefente my Schoole, my cunning, and my felfe to your worthy Patronage. Befeeching you,
though I bidde you to Dinner,
not to looke for a feaft fit for the
curious tafte of a perfect Cour-
tier : but too imitate Philip of
Macedon, who beeing inuited
to a Farmers houfe, when hee
came from Hunting, brought a
greater trayne than the poore
man looked for: When they
were fette, the good Philip per-
ceiuing his Hofte forowfull, for
want of meate to fatiffie fo many, exhorted his friends to keepe
their ftomackes for the fetonde
courfe: wherevppon euery man
fedde

.edde modeſtly on that whiche
ſtoode before him , and leſte
meate inough at the taking vppe
of the table. And I truſt if your
Worſhippe feede ſparingly on
this, (too comforte your poore
Hoſte) in hope of a better courſe
heereafter, though the Diſhes be
fewe, that I ſet before you,
they ſhall for this time
ſuffice your ſelfe
& a great ma-
ny moe.

Your Worſhippes to
commaund, *Stephan
Goſſon.*

Entlemen, and others, you may wel thinke that I sell you my corne, and eate Chaffe; batrer my wine, & drinke Water; sith I take vpon mee to driue you from Playes, when mine owne woorkes are dayly to be seene vpon stages, as sufficient witnesses of mine owne folly, and seuere Iudges againste my selfe. But if you sawe how many teares of sorrowe mine eyes shed, when I beholde them; or how many drops of blood my heart sweates, when I remember them; you would not so much blame me for misspending my time, when I knew not what I did; as commend mee at the laste, for recouering my steppes, with grauer counsell. After-wittes are euer best, burnt Children dread the fire, I haue seene that which you behold, & I shun that which you frequent.

frequent. And that I might the eafier pull your mindes from fuch ftudyes, drawe your feete from fuch places; I haue fente you a Schoole of thofe abufes, which I haue gathered by obferuation.

Theodorus the Atheift complayned, that his fchollers were woont, how plaine foeuer he fpake, to mifconfter him; howe right foeuer hee wrote, to wreft him: And I looke for fome fuch Auditors in my Schoole, as of rancour will hit me, how foeuer I warde; or of ftomake affayle mee, how foeuer I bee garded; making black of white, Chalke of Cheefe, the full Moone of a meffe of Cruddes. Thefe are fuch as with curft Curres barke at euery man but their owne friendes : thefe fnatch vp bones in open ftreetes, and byte them with madneffe in fecrete corners : thefe with fharpe windes, pearce fubtiler in narrowe lanes then in large fieldes. And fith there is neither authoritie in

me

me to bridle their tongues, nor reason in them to rule their owne talke;
I am contented to suffer their taunts;
requesting you which are Gentlemē,
of curtesie to beare with me, and because you are learned amende the
faultes freendly, which escape the
Presse : The ignoraunt I knowe
will swallow them downe,
and digest them with
case. Farewel.

Yours Stephan
Gosson.

HE Syracuſans b-
ſed ſuch varietie of
diſhes in theyr ban-
quets, that when
they were ſette, and
their boozdes furni-
ſhed, they were ma-
ny times in doubt, which they ſhoulde
touch firſt, oz taſte laſt. And in my opinion the wozlde giueth euery wziter ſo
large a fielde to walke in, that befoze he
ſet penne to the booke, he ſhall finde him
ſelfe feaſted at Syracuſa, vncertaine
where to begin, oz when to end. This
cauſed Pindarus too queſtion with his
Muſe, whether be were better with his
art to diſciſer the life of ẙ Nimpe Me-
lia, oz Cadmus encoũter with the Dra-
gon, oz the warres of Hercules, at the
walles of Thebes, oz Bacchus cuppes,
oz Venus tugling. Hee ſawe ſo many

A   turnings

turninges layde open to his feete, that hee knewe not which way to bende his pace.

Therfore as I cannot but cōmende his wisedome, whiche in banqueting feedes most vpon that, that doth nourish best; so must I dispraise his methode in writing, which following the course of amarous Poets, dwelleth longest in those pointes, that profite least; and like a wanton whelpe, leaueth the game, to runne riot. The Scarabe flies ouer many a sweete flower, & lightes in a cowshard: It is the custome of the fire to leaue the sound places of the Horse, and suck at the Botch: The nature of Colloquintida, to draw the worst humours too it selfe: The maner of Swine, to forsake the fayre fieldes, and wallow in the myre: And the whole practise of Poets, eyther with fables to shew theyr abuses, or with plaine tearmes to vnfold theyr mischiefe, discouer theyr shame, discredit them selues, and disperse their poyson through all the worlde. Virgill sweates in describyng his Gnat: Ouid bestirred bestirreth him to paint out his Flea: the one shewes his art in the lust of Dido, the other his cunning in the inceste of Myrrha, and that trumpet of Baudrie, the Craft of loue.

I must confesse that Poets are the whetstones of wit, notwithstanding that wit is dearly bought: where hony and gall are mixed, it will be hard to seuer the one from the other. The deceitfull Phisition giueth sweete Syropes to make his poyson goe downe the smoother: The Iuggler casteth a myst to worke the closer: The Syrens song is the Saylers wracke: The Fowlers whistle, the birdes death: The wholesome bayte, the fishes bane: The Harpies haue Virgins faces, and vultures Talentes: Hyena speakes like a friend, & deuoures like a Foe: The calmest Seas hide dangerous Rockes: the Woolfe iettes in Weathers felles: Many good sentences are spoken by Dauus, to shadowe his knauery: and written by Poets, as ornamentes to beautifye their woorkes, and sette

their

theyr trumperie too sale without suspect.

But if you looke well too Epæus horse, you shall finde in his bowels the destruction of Troy: open the sepulchre of Semyramis, whose Title promiseth suche wealth to the Kinges of Persia, you shall see nothing but deate bones: Rippe vp the golden Ball, that Nero consecrated to Jupiter Capitollinus, you shall haue it stuffed with the shauinges of his Beard: pul off the visard that Poets maske in, you shall disclose their reproch, bewray their vanitie, loth their wantonnesse, lament their follie, and perceiue their sharpe sayings to be placed as Pearles in Dunghils, fresh pictures on rotten walles, chaste Matrons apparel on common Curtesans. These are the Cuppes of Circes, that turne reasonable Creatures into brute Beastes; the balles of Hippomenes, that hinder the course of Atalanta; and the blocks of the Diuel that are cast in our wayes, to cut off the race of toward wittes. No marueyle though Plato

shut

ſhut them out of his Schoole, and bani-
ſhed them quite from his common
wealth, as effeminate writers, vnprofi-
table members, and vtter enimies to
vertue.

The Romans were verie deſirous
to imitate the Greekes, and yet verie
loth to receiue their Poets : inſomuch
that Cato layth it in the diſhe of Marcus the noble as a foule reproche, that
in the time of his Conſulſhippe, hee
brought Ennius the Poet into his pro-
uince. Tullie accuſtomed to read them
with great diligence in his youth, but
when hee waxed grauer in ſtudie, elder
in yeares, riper in iudgement, hee ac-   *Tuſc 1.2.*
cōpted them the fathers of lyes, Pipes
of vanitie, & Schooles of Abuſe. Maximus Tyrius taketh vppon him to de-
fend the diſcipline of theſe Doctors vnder the name of Homer, wreſting the
raſhnes of Aiax, to valour; the cowardice
of Vliſſes, to Pollicie; the dotage of Ne-
ſtor, to graue counſell ; and the battaile
of Troy, too the woonderfull conflict of
the foure Clementes : where Iuno

       A 3   which

which is counted the ayꝛc, settes in her
foote to take vp the strife,& steps boldly
betwixt them to part the fray. It is a
Pageant wooꝛth the sight, to beholde
how he labors w̔ Mountaines to bꝛing
fooꝛth Mise ; much like to some of those
Players, that come to the scaffold with
Dꝛum & Trumpet to pꝛoser skirmishe,
and when they haue sounded Allarme, off
go the peeces to encounter a shadow, oꝛ
conquere a Paper monster. You will
smile I am sure if you read it, to see how
this moꝛall Philosopher toyles too
dꝛaw the Lyons skin vpon Æsops Asse.
Hercules shoes on a childes feete, a im-
plyfying that which the moꝛe it is stir-
red, the moꝛe it stinker; he lesse it is talked of, the better it is liked; & as way-
warde childꝛen, the moꝛe they bee flate-
red, the woꝛse they are; oꝛ as curst soꝛes
with often touching waxe angry, & run
the longer without healing. He attributeth the beginning of vertue to Miner-
ua, of friendship to Venus, & the roote
of all handy crafts to Vulcan; but if he
had bꝛoke his arme aswel as his legge,
                                        when

when he fel out of heauen into Lemnos,
either Apollo must haue played the
Bonesetter, oz euery occupation beene
laide a water. Plato when he sawe the
doctrine of these Teachers, neither foz Poets banished by Plato,
pzofite, necessary, noz to be wished foz
pleasure, gaue them all Drumics enter-
tainment, not suffering the once to shew
their faces in a refozmed common wealth.
And the same Tyrius that layes such a
scituation foz Poets, in the name of Homer, ouerthzows his whole building in
the person of Mithecus, which was an
excellent Cooke among the Greekes, &
asmuch honozed foz his confections, as
Phidias foz his caruing. But when he
came to Sparta, thinking there foz his
cunning to be accusted a God, the good
lawes of Licurgus, & custom of the country were to hot foz his diet. The gouer-
nozs banished him & his art, & al the in-
habitants folowing the steppes of their
Predecessozs, vsed not with daynties to
prouoke appetite, but with labour and
trauell too whette their stomackes to
their meate.   I may well liken Ho-

Poetes and
Cooker compared togither.

mer to Mithecus, & Poets to Cookes
the pleasures of the one winnes the body frō labor, & conquereth the sense; the
allurcmēt of the other drawes the mind
from vertue, and confoundeth wit. As
in euery perfect common wealth there
ought to be good laws established, right
mainteined, wrong repressed, vertue rewarded, vice punished, and all maner of
abuses thoroughly purged: So ought
there such schooles for the furtherance
of the same to be aduaunced, that young
men maye bee taught that in greene
peeres, that becomes them to practise
in gray haires.

Poetrie in
Scythia without
vice, as the
Phœnix in Arabia, without a
fellow.

Anacharsis beeing demaunded of
a Grecke, whether they had not instrumentes of Musicke, or Schooles of
Poetrie in Scythia, answered, yea, and
that without vice, as though it were either impossible, or incredible, that no abuse should be learned where such lessōs
are taught, & such schooles mainteined.

Salust in describing the nurture
of Sempronia, commendeth her witte
in that shee coulde frame her selfe to
all

all companies, too talke discretely with
wyse men, and vaynely with wantons;
taking a quip ere it came too grounde,
and returning it back without a faulte.
She was taught (saith he) both Greek
and Latine, she coulde versifie, sing, and
daunce, better then became an honest
woman. Sappho was skilfull in Poetrie and sung wel, but she was whorish.
I set not this downe too condemne the
giftes of versifying, daunsing, or sing-
yng in women, so they bee vsed with
meane, & exercised in due tyme. But to
shew you that as by Anacharsis report
the Scythians did it without offence: so
one Swalowe bringes not Sommer;
nor one particular example sufficient
proofe for a generall precept. Whyte
siluer, drawes a blacke lyne; Fyre is as
hurtfull, as healthie; Water as daun-
gerous, as it is commodious; and these
qualities as harde to bee wel vsed when
we haue them, as they are to be learned
before wee get them. Hee that goes to
Sea, must smel of the Ship; and that
sayles into Poets wil sauour of Pitch.

Qualities al-
lowed in wo-
men.

C. Marius

C. Marius in the assembly of the whole Senate at Rome, in a solemne oration, giueth an account of his bringing vp: he sheweth that he hath beene taught to lye on the ground, to suffer all weathers, to leaue men, to strike his foe, to feare nothing but an euill name : and chalengeth praise vnto him selfe, in that hee neuer learned the Greeke tongue, neither ment to be instructed in it heerafter, either that he thought it too farre a iorney to fetche learning beyonde the fielde, or because he doubted the abuses of those Schooles, where Poets were euer the head Maisters. Tiberius the Emperour sawe somewhat, when he iudged Scaurus to death for writing a Tragidie : Augustus, when hee banished Ouid : And Nero when he charged Lucan, to put vp his pipes, to stay his penne and write no more. Burrus and Seneca the schoolemaisters of Nero are flowted and hated of the people, for teaching their Scholer the song of Attis. For Dion saith, that the hearing thereof wroonge laughter and teares from

Poets chiefe
Maisters in
Greece.

Poets banished frō Rome.

Dion in vita
Neronis.

from most of those that were then aboue
him. Wherby I iudge that they scorned
the folly of the teachers, and lamented
the frenzie of the Scholer, who beeing
Emperour of Rome, and bearing the
weight of the whole common wealth
vppon his shoulders, was easier to bee
drawen to vanitie by wanton Poets,
then to good gouernment by the father-
ly counsell of graue Senators. They
were condemned to dye by the lawes of
the Heathens , which inchaunted the
graine in other mens grounds: and are
not they accursed thinke you by the
mouth of God, which hauing the gouernment of young Princes , with Poeticall fatalies draw them to the schooles
of their owne abuses , bewitching the
graine in the greene blade , that was
sowed for the sustenance of many thousands, & poisoning the spring with their
amorous lapes, whence the whole common wealth should fetch water? But to
leaue the scepter to Iupiter, and instructing of Princes to Plutarch and Xe-
nophon I will beare a lowe sayle, and
                                            row'e

rowe neere the shore, least I chaunce
to bee carried beyonde my reache, or
runne a grounde in those Coasts which
I neuer knewe . My onely endeuour
shalbe to shew you that in a rough cast,
which I see in a cloude, loking through
my fingers.

And because I haue bene matricula-
ted my selfe in the schoole, where so many abuses florish, I wil imitate ý dogs
of Ægypt, which cōming to the bancks
of Nylus too quenche their thirste, syp
and away, drinke running, lest they bee
snapte short for a pray too Crocodiles.
I shoulde tel tales out of the Schoole,
and bee Ferruled for my faulte, or
hyssed at for a blab, yf I layde al the
orders open before your eyes. You are
no sooner entred, but libertie looseth the
reynes, and geues you head, placing
you with Poetrie in the lowest former
when his skill is showne too make his
Scholer as good as euer twangde, bee
preferres you too Pyping, from Pyping to playing, from play to pleasure,
from pleasure to slouth, from slouth too
sleepe,

sleepe, from sleepe too sinne, from sinne to death, from death to the deuill, if you take your learning apace, and passe through euery forme without reuolting. Looke not too haue mee discourse these at large, the Crocodile watcheth to take me tardie, whichsoeuer of them I touche, is a byle: Trype and goe, for I dare not tarry.

Heraclides accounteth Amphyon the ringleader of Poets and Pypers: Delphus Philammones penned the birth of Latona, Diana, & Apollo in verse; and taught the people to Pype & Daunce rounde about the Temple of Delphos. Hesiodus was as cunning in Pyping, as in Poetrie: so was Terpandrus, and after him Clonas. Apollo which is honoured of Poets as the God of their Art, had at the one side of his Idol in Delos a Bowe, and at the other, the three Graces with three sundrie instruments, of which one was a pype, and some writers affirme that he pyped himselfe now and than.

Poetrie and pyping, haue allwaies beene

bene so vnited togither, that til the time of Melanippides, Pipers were Poets hyerlings. But marke I pray you, how they are nowe both abused.

The right vse of auncient Poetrie was too haue the notable exploytes of woorthy Captaines, the holesome councels of good fathers, and vertuous liues of predecessors set downe in nunters, and song to the Instrument at solemne feastes, that the sound of the one might draw the hearers from kissing the cupp too often, the sense of the other put them in minde of things past, and chaulk out the way to do the like. After this maner were the Bœotians trained from rudenesse to ciuilitie, The Lacedæmonians instructed by Tyrtæus verse, The Argiues by the melody of Telesilla, And the Lesbians by Alcæus Odes.

To this end are instruments vsed in battaile, not to tickle the eare, but too teach euery souldier when to strike and when to stay, when to flye, and when to followe. Chiron by singing to his instrument, quencheth Achiles furye :

Terpandrus

Terpandrus with his notes, layeth
the tempeſt, and pacifies the tumult at
Lacedæmon: Homer with his Muſicke cured the ſick Souldiers in the
Grecians campe, and purged euery
mans Tent of the Plague. Thinke
you that thoſe miracles coulde bee
wꝛought with playing of Daunces,
Dumpes, Pauins, Galiardes, Mea-
ſures Fancyes, oꝛ new ſtreynes? They
neuer came wher this grewe, noꝛ knew
what it ment.

Pythagoras bequeathes them a
Clookebagge, and condemnes them
foꝛ fooles, that iudge Muſicke by
ſounde and eare. If you will bee
good Scholers, and pꝛofite well in the
Arte of Muſicke, ſhutte your Fidels in
their caſes, and looke vp to heauen: the
oꝛder of the Spheres, the vnfallible
motion of the Planets, the iuſte courſe
of the yeere, and barietie of ſeaſons,
the concoꝛde of the Elementes and
their qualyties, Fyre, Water, Ayꝛe,
Earth, Heate, Colde, Moyſture and
Dꝛought concurring togeather to the
coꝛy

constitution of earthly bodies and sustenance of euery creature.

The politike Lawes, in well go-
uerned common wealthes, that treade
downe the prowde, and vpholde the
meeke, the loue of the King & his sub-
iectes, the Father and his childe, the
Lorde and his Slaue, the Maister
and his Man, The Trophees and
Triumphes of oure auncestours, which
pursued vertue at the harde heeles, and
shunned vyce as a rocke for feare of
shipwracke, are excellent maisters too
shewe you that this is right Musicke,
this perfecte harmony. Chiron when
hee appcased the wrath of Achilles,
tolde him the duetie of a good souldier,
repeated the vertues of his father Pe-
leus, and sung the famous enterprises
of noble men. Terpandrus when he ended the brabbles at Lacedæmon, neyther pyped Rogero nor Turkelony,
but reckoning vp the commodities of
friendeship, and fruites of debate, putting them in mind of Lycurgus lawes,
taught them too treade a better measure.

When Homers muſicke droue the pe-
ſtilence from the Grecians camp, there
was no ſuch vertue in his penne, nor in
his pipe, but if I might bee vmpier, in
the ſweet harmony of diuerſe natures &
wonderful concord of ſundry medicines.
For Apolloes cunning extendeth it ſelf
aſwel to Phiſick, as muſick or Poetrie.
And Plutarch reporteth that as Chiron was a wiſe man, a learned Poet, a
ſkilful Muſition, ſo was hee alſo a
teacher of iuſtice, by ſhewing what
Princes ought to doe, and a Reader of
Phiſicke, by opening the natures of
manie ſimples. If you enquire howe
manie ſuche Poetes and Pipers wee
haue in our Age, I am perſwaded that
euerie one of them may creepe through
a ring, or daunce the wilde Morice in
a Needles eye. We haue infinite Poets, and Pipers, and ſuche peeuiſhe
cattel among vs in Englande, that liue
by merrie begging, mainteyned by
almes, and priuily encroch vppon euerie mans purſe. But if they that are in
authoritie, and haue the ſworde in their
handes to cut off abuſes, ſhoulde call an

B   ac-

accōpt to see how many Chirons, Ter-
pandri, and Homers are heere, they
might cast the summe without pen, or
counters, and sit downe with Racha, to
weepe for her Children, because they
were not. He that compareth our instruments, with those that were vsed in ancient times, shall see them agree like
Dogges & Cattes, and meete as rump
as Germans lippes. Terpandrus and
Olimpus vsed instrumēts of 7. strings.
And Plutarch is of opinion that the instruments of 3. strings, wͧ were vsed before their time, passed al that haue followed since. It was an old law & lōg kept
that no mā should according to his owne
humor, adde or diminish, in matters cō-
cerningthat Art, but walk in the pathes
of their predecessors. But whē newfan-
gled Phrynis becam a fidler, being som-
what curious in carping, & searching for
moats wͧ a pair of blearde eies, thought
to amend his maisters, & marred al. Timotheus a bird of the same broode, & a
right hosd of the same Hare, toke the 7.
stringed harp, that was altogether vsed
in Terpādrus time, & increaced the num
ber

ber of the strings at his owne pleasure.
The Argiues appointed by their lawes
great punishments for such as placed a-
boue 7.strings vpō any instrument. Pythagoras cōmaunded that no Musition
should go beyond his Diapason. Were
the Argiues & Pythagoras nowe aliue,
& saw how many frets, how many strin-
ges, how many stops, how many keyes,
how many cliffes, howe many moodes,
how many flats, how many sharps, how
many rules, how many spaces, how many noates, how many restes, how many
querks, how many corners, what chop-
ping, what chāging, what tossing, what
turning, what wresting & wringing is
among our Musitions, I beleue verily,
that they would cry out with the coūtry
man: *Hen quòd tam pingui macer est
mihi taurus in aruo.* Alas here is fat fee-
ding, & leane beasts: or as one said at the
shearing of hogs, great cry & litle wool,
much adoe, & smal help. To shew y abuses of these vnthrifty scholers that des-
pise y good rules of their anciēt masters
& run to the shop of their owne deuises,

defacing olde ſtampes, foꝛging newe
Pꝛintes, and coining ſtrange pꝛecepts,
Phærecrates a Comicall Poet, bꝛin-
geth in Muſicke and Juſtice vpon the
ſtage : Muſicke with her clothes tot-
tered, her fleſhe toꝛne, her face defoꝛ-
med, her whole bodie mangled and diſ-
membꝛed : Juſtice, viewing her well,
and pitying her caſe, queſtioneth with
her howe ſhee came in that plight : to
whom Muſick replyes, that Melanippides, Phrynis Timotheus, & ſuch fan-
taſticall heades, haue ſo disfigured her
lookes, defaced her beautie, ſo hacked
her, and hewed her, and with manye
ſtringes, geuen her ſo many woundes,
that ſhe is ſtriken to death, in daunger
to periſhe, and preſent in place the leaſt
part of her ſelfe. When the Sicilians,
and Dores foꝛſooke the playnſong that
they had learned of their auunceſtours in
the Mountaynes, and pꝛactiſed long a-
mong theyꝛ heardes, they founde out
ſuch deſcant in Sybaris inſtrumentes,
that by daunſing and ſkipping they
fel into lewdneſſe of life. Neither ſtaied
theſe

Muſicke ſoꝛe
wounded.

these abuses in the compasse of that countrey: but like vnto yll weedes in time spread so far, that they choked the good grayne in euery place.

For as Poetrie & Piping are Cosen germans: so piping, and playing are of great affinity, and all three chayned in linkes of abuse.

Plutarch complaineth, that ignorant men, not knowyng the maiestie of auncient musick, abuse both the eares of the people, and the Arte it selfe: with bringing sweete consortes into Theaters, which rather effeminate the minde, as prickes vnto vice, then procure amendement of maners, as spurres to vertue. Ouid the high martial of Venus fielde planteth his maine battell in publique assemblies, sendeth out his scoutes too Theaters to descry the enimie, and in steede of vaunt Curriers, with instruments of musicke, playing, singing, and dauncing, geues the first charge. Maximus Tyrius holdeth it for a Maxime, that the bringing of instrumets to Theaters & plaies, was the first cup that poi

B3   soned

ned the common weaith. They that are
bozne in Seriphos, & cockered cōtinual-
ly in those Islandes, where they see nothing but Foxes, & Hares, wil neuer be
persuaded that there are huger beastes:
They that neuer went out of the chāpi-
ons in Brabant , will hardly conceiue
what rockes are in Germany. And they
that neuer goe out of their houses , for
regard of their credit, noz steppe from
the vniuersitye for loue of knowledge,
seeing but slender offences & small abuses within their owne walles ,wil neuer
beleeue ẏ such rockes are abrode , noz
such hozrible monsters in playing places . But as (I speake the one to my
comforte, the other to my shame , and
remember both with a sozrowfull hart)
I was first instructed in the vniuersity ,
after drawne like a nouice to these abu-
ses:so wil I shew you what I see, & in-
forme you what I reade of such affaires.
Ouid sayth, that Romulus builte his
Theater as a horse faire for hozes,made
Triumphes,& set out playes to gather
the fayze women togither , that euery
one of his souldiers might take where
                                        he

be liked, a snatch for his share: wherupon the Amarous Scholemaister burſteth out in these words:

Romule, militib' solus dare præmia noſti:
  Hæc mihi si dederis cōmoda, miles ero.

Thou Romulus alone knoweſt how
  thy ſouldiers to rewarde:
Graunt me the like, my ſelſe will be
  attendant on thy garde.

It ſhould ſeeme that the abuſe of ſuch places was ſo great, that for any chaſte liuer to haunt them was a black ſwan, & a white crowe. Dion ſo ſtraightly forbiddeth the ancient families of Rome & gentlewomen that tender their name & honor, to che to Theaters, & rebuks thē ſo ſharply, when he takes thē napping, that if they be but once ſeene there, hee iudgeth it ſufficient cauſe to ſpeake il of them & thinke worſe. The ſhadowe of a knaue hurts an honeſt mā: the ſent of the ſtewes a ſober matron: and the ſhew of Theaters a ſimple gaſer. Clitomachus the wreſtler geuen altogether to manly exerciſe, if hee had hearde any talke of loue, in what cōpany ſoeuer he had bin,

woulu

would forſake his ſeat, & bid them adue;

Lacon when bee ſawe the Atheni-
ens ſtudie ſo muche to ſet out Playes,
ſayde they were madde . If men foz
good exerciſe , and women for theyr
credite, be ſhut from Theaters, whom
ſhal we ſuffer to goe thither? Litle childzen? Plutarch with a caueat keepeth
them out, not ſo much as admitting the
litle crackhalter that carrieth his mai-
ſters pantouffles , to ſet foote within
thoſe doores: And alledgeth this reaſõ,
that thoſe wanton ſpectacles of lyght
huſwiues, dzawing gods from the heauens,& young men from them ſelues to
ſhipwzacke of honeſtie, will hurte them
moze, thẽ if at the Epicures table, they
had nigh burſt their guts with ouer fee-
ding. For if the body bee ouercharged,
it may bee holpe; but the ſurfite of the
ſoule is hardly cured. Here I doubt not

Obiection.

but ſome Archplayer oz other that hath
read alitle, oz ſtumbled vp chance vpon
Plautus comedies, wil call me a bone oz
it to pick, ſaying, ÿ whatſoeuer theſe ancient wziters haue ſpokẽ againſt plaies
is

is to bee applied too the abuses in olde
Comedies, where Gods are broughte
in, as Prisoners too beautie, rauishers
of Virgins, and seruantes by loue, too
earthly creatures. But the Comedies
that are exercised in oure daies are better sifted. They shewe no such branne:
The first smelte of Plautus, these tast of
Menäder; the lewdenes of Gods, is al-
tred and chaunged to the loue of young
men; force, to friendshippe; rapes, too
mariage; wooing allowed by assu-
rance of wedding; priuie meetinges of
bachelours and maidens on the stage,
not as murderers that deuour the good
name eeh of other in their mindes, but,
as those that desire to bee made one in
hearte. Nowe are the abuses of the
worlde reuealed, euery man in a playl
may see his owne faultes, and learne:
by this glasse, to amende his manners.
Curculio may chatte til his heart ake,)
ere any be offended with his gybes.
Deformities are checked in ieast, and
mated in earnest. The sweetenesse of
musicke, and pleasure of sportes, tem-
B 5 per

per the bitternesse of rebukes, and miti-
tigate the tartenesse of euery taunt ac-
cozding to this.

Omne vafer vitiũ ridens Flaccus amice
Narrat, & admissus circũ p̃cordia ludit.

<small>Flaccus</small> among his friends, with fanning Muse
Doth nip him neere, that foistreth foule abuse:

Some Quere.

    Therefoze they are either so blinde,
that they cannot, oz so blunt, that they
will not see why this exercise shoulde
not be suffered as a pzofitable recreation. Foz my parte I am neither so fonde
a Phisition, noz so bad a Cooke, but I
can allowe my patient a cup of wine to
meales, although it be hotte; and pleasaunt sauces to dziue downe his meate,
if his stomake bee queasie. Notwithstanding, if people will bee instructed,
(God be thanked) wee haue Diuines
enough to discharge that, and moe by a
great many, then are well harkened to:
yet sith these abuses are growne too
head, and sinne so rype, the number is
                              lesse

lesse then I would it were.

Euripides holdes not him onely a foole, that beeing well at home, wil gad abzode, that hath a Conduite within doore, and fetcheth water without: but all suche beside, as haue sufficient in them selues, to make them selues merry with pleasaunte talke, tending too good, and mixed with ἐυτραπελία the Grecians glee, yet will they seeke when they neede not, to bee spozted abzode at playes and Pageauntes. Plutarch likeneth the recreation that is gotte by conference, too a pleasaunt banquet; the sweet pappe of the one suſtaineth the body, the sauery doctrine of the other doth nouriſh the minde: and as in banquetting, the wayter ſtandes ready too fill the Cuppe: So in all our recreations we ſhoulde haue an inſtructer at our elbowes to feede the ſoule. If wee gather Grapes among thiſtles, oz ſeeke foz this foode at Theaters, wee ſhall haue a harde pyttaunce, and come to ſhozte commons. I cannot thinke that Cittie to be ſafe,
                                                    that

that strikes downe her Percollices,
rammes vp her gates, and suffereth the
enimie to enter the posterne. Neyther
wil I be perswaded, that he is any way
likely to conquer affection, which brea-
keth his instrumentes, burneth all his
Poets, abandons his haunt, muffleth his
eyes as he passeth the streate, and re-
sortes too Theaters too bee assaulted.
Cookes did neuer shewe more crafte in
their iunckets to vanquish the taste, nor
Painters in shadowes to allure the eye,
then Poets in Theaters to wounde the
conscience.

 There setthey abroche straunge
consortes of melody, to tickle the eare;
costly apparel, to flatter the sight; effeminate gesture, to rauish the sence; and
wanton speache, to whet desire too in-
ordinate lust. Therefore of both bar-
relles, I iudge Cookes and Painters
the better hearing, for the one extendeth
his arte no farther then to the tongue,
palate, and nose, the other to the eye;
and both are ended in outwarde sense,
which is common too vs with bruite
        beastes.

beasts. But these by the priuie entries of the eare, slip downe into the hart, & with gunshotte of affection gaule the minde, where reason and vertue should rule the roste . These people in Rome were as pleasant as Nectar at the first beginning, & cast out for lees, when their abuses were knowen. They whome Cæsar vpheld, were driuen out by Octauian : whom Caligula reclaimed, were cast of by Nero : whom Neruä exalted, were throwne downe by Traian : whom Anthony admitted, were expelled againe, pestred in Gallies & sent into Hellespōt by Marcus Aurelius. But when the whole rabble of Poets, Pipers, Players, Jugglers, Jesters, & daūcers were receiued againe, Rome was reported to bee fuller of fooles then of wise men. Domitian suffered playing & dauncing so long in Theaters, that Paris led the shaking of sheetes with Domitia, and Mnesterthe Trenchmour with Messalina. Caligula made so muche of Players and Daunters, that hee suffered them openly to kysse his lyppes,

Domitia was the first wife of Domitian, and Messalina, the seconde.

Dion

when the Senators might scarce haue
a lick at his feete: He gaue Dauncers
great stipends for selling their hopps:
& placed Apelles the player by his own
sweete side: Besides that you may see
what excellent graue men were euer a-
bout him, he loued Prasinus the Coch-
man so wel, that for good wil to the master, he bid his horse to supper, gaue him
wine to drink in cups of estate, set barly
graines of golde before him to eate, and
swore by no bugs, that hee would make
him a Consul: which thing (saith Dion)
had bin performed, had hee not bin pre-
uented by suddain death. For as his life
was abhominable, so was his end miserable: Comming from dancing & playing, he was slaine by Chærea, a iust rewarde, and a fit Catastrophe. I haue
heard some Players vaunt of the credit
they had in Rome, but they are as foolish in that, as Vibius Rufus which boo-
sted himself to be an Emperor because
hee had sit in Cæsars chaire, & a perfect
Orator, because hee was marryed to
Tullies widowe. Better might they say
them

them selues to be murderers, because
they haue represented the persons of
Thyestes and Atreus, Achilles & He-
ctor: or perfect Limme listers, for teaching the trickes of euery Strumpet.
Such are the abuses that I reade of in
Rome: such are the Caterpillers that
haue deuoured and blasted the fruite of
Ægypt: Such are the Dragons that
are hurtful in Affricke : Such are the
Adders that sting with pleasure, and kil
with paine: and such are the Basiliskes
of the world, that poyson, as well with
the beame of their sighte, as with the
breath of their mouth.

Consider with thy selfe (gentle Reader) the olde discipline of Englande,
mark what we were before, & what we
are now: Leaue Rome a while, and cast
thine eye backe to thy Predecessors,
and tell mee howe woonderfully wee
haue beene chaunged, since wee were
schooled with these abuses. Dion sayth,
that english men could suffer watching
and labor, hunger & thirst, and beare of
al stormes w head and shoulders, they v-
sed

Maners of
England in
olde time,

sed slender weapons, went naked, and
were good soldiours, they fed vppon
rootes and barkes of trees, they would
stand vp to the chin many dayes in ma-
rishes without victualles: and they had
a kind of sustenaunce in time of neede,
of which if they had take but the quan-
titie of a beane, or the weight of a pease,
they did neyther gape after meate, nor
long for the cuppe, a great while after.

Olde exercise
of England.
The men in valure not yeelding to Sci-
thia, the women in courage passing the
Amazons. The exercise of both was
shootyng and darting, running & wre-
stling, and trying suche maisteries, as
eyther consisted in swiftnesse of feete, a-
gilitie of body, strength of armes, or
New England Martiall discipline. But the exercise
that is nowe among vs, is banqueting,
playing, pipyng, and dauncing, and all
suche delightes as may win vs to pleasure, or rocke vs a sleepe.

Oh what a woonderfull chaunge
is this? Our wrastling at armes, is
turned to wallowyng in Ladies laps,
our courage, to cowardice, our running
to

to ryot, our Bowes into Bolles, and our Dartes to Dishes.   We haue robbed Greece of Gluttonie, Italy of wantonnesse, Spaine of pride, Fraunce of deceite, and Dutchland of quaffing. Compare London to Rome, & England to Italy, you shall finde the Theaters of the one, the abuses of the other, to be rife among vs. *Experto crede*, I haue seene somewhat, and therefore I thinke may say the more.   In Rome when Plaies or Pageants are showne; Ouid chargeth his Pilgrims, to crepe close to the Saintes, whom they serue, and shew their double diligence to lifte the Gentlewomens roabes from the grounde, for soyling in the rusle; to sweepe Moates from their Kirtles, to keepe their fingers in vre; to lay their hands at their backes for an easie slap; to looke vppon those, whome they beholde; too prayse that, whiche they commende; too lyke euerye thing, that pleaseth them; to presente them Pomegranates, to picke as they syt, and when all is done, to waite on them,

C.   maner-

mannerly too their houses. In our assemblies at playes in London, you shall see suche heauing, and shoouing, suche ytching and shouldring, too sitte by women; Suche care for their garments, that they bee not trode on: Such eyes to their lappes, that no chippes light in them: Such ptillowes to ther backes, that they take no hurte: Such masking in their eares, I knowe not what: Such giuing them Pippins to passe the time: Sucke playing at foote Saunt without Cardes: Such ticking, such toying, such smiling, such winking, and such maning them home, when the sportes are ended, that it is a right Comedie, to marke their behauiour, to watche their conceites, as the Catte for the Mouse, and as good as a course at the game it selfe, to dogge them a little, or followe aloofe by the print of their feete, and so discouer by flotte where the Deare taketh soyle. If this were as well noted, as ill seene: or as openly punished, as secretly practised: I haue no doubts but the cause would

would be feared to d2y vp the effect, and
these p2ettie Rabbe:s very cunningly
ferretted from their bo2rowes . Fo2
they that lack Cuſtomers al the weeke,
either becauſe their haunte is vnkno-
wen, o2 the Conſtables and Officers of
their Pariſhe, watch them ſo narrowly,
that they dare not queatche; To cele-
b2ate the Sabboth, flock to Theaters,
and there keepe a generall Market of
Bawd2ie: Not that any filthyneſſe in
deede, is committed within the com-
paſſe of that grounde, as was doone in
Rome, but that euery wanton and his
Paramour, euery man and his Miſ-
treſſe, euery John and his Joan, euery
knaue and his queane, are there firſt acquainted ⁊ cheapen the Merchandiſe
in that place, which they pay fo2 elſe
where as they can agree . Theſe
wo2mes when they dare not neſtle in
the Peſcod at home, finde refuge ab2ode
and are hidde in the eares of other
mens Co2ne. Euery Uawter in one
blinde Tauerne o2 other, is Tenant at
will, to which ſhee tolleth reſo2te, and

C, 2,   playes

playes the ſtale to vtter their victualls, and helpe them to emptie their muſtie caſkes. There is ſhe ſo intreated with wordes, and receiued with curteſie, that euery back roome in the houſe is at her commaundement. Some that haue neither land to maintaine them, nor good occupation to get their breade, deſirous to ſtrowt it with the beſte, yet diſdayning too liue by the ſweate of their browes, haue found out this caſt of Ledgerdemayne, to play faſt & looſe among their neighbours. If any parte of Muſick haue ſuffred ſhipwrack, and ariued by fortune at their fingers endes, with ſhewe of gentilitie they take vp faire houſes, receiue luſty laſſes at a price for boorders, and pipe from morning to euening for wood and coale. By the brothers, coſens, vncles, great grandſires, and ſuche like acquaintaunce of their gheſtes, they drink of the beſt, they ſit rente free, they haue their owne Table ſpreade to their handes, without wearing the ſtrings of their purſſe, or any thing elſe , but houſholde and honeſty.

neſtie. When reſorte ſo increaſeth that they growe in ſuſpicion, and the pottes which are ſent ſo often too the Tauerne, gette ſuch a knock before they come home, that they returne their Mayſter a crack to his credite: Though hee bee called in queſtion of his life, hee hath ſhiftes inoughe to auoyde the blanke. If their houſes bee ſearched, ſome inſtrumente of Muſick is layde in ſighte to dazell the eyes of euery Officer, and all that are lodged in the houſe by night, or frequente it by day, come thither as pupilles to be well ſchoolde. Other ther are which beeing ſo knowen that they are the by-woorde of euery mans mouth, and pointed at commonly as they paſſe the ſtreetes, either couch them ſelues in Alpes, or blind Lanes, or take ſanctuary in ſryeries, or liue a mile from the Cittie like Venus Nunnes in a Cloyſter at Newington, Ratliffe, Iſlington, Hogſdon or ſome ſuch place, where like penitents, they deny the worlde, and ſpende theyr dayes in double

deuotion

deuotion. And when they are weery of
contemplation to comfort themselues,
and renue their acquaintaunce, they vi-
sit Theaters, where they make full account of a pray before they departe, Solon made no lawe for Parricides, because he feared that hee shoulde rather
put men in minde to commit such offences, then by any straunge punishment,
giue them a bitte to keepe them vnder.
And I intende not to shewe you al that
I see, nor halfe that I heare of these a-
buses, lest you iudge me more wilfull to
teach them, then willing to forbid them.

I looke still when Players shoulde
cast me their Gauntlets, and challenge
a combate for entring so far into their
possessions, as though I made them
Lords of this misrule, or the very schol-
maisters of these abuses: though the
best Clarkes bee of that opinion, they
beare not me say so. There are more
houses then Parishe Churches, more
maydes then Maulkin, more wayes
to the woode then one, and more causes
in nature then Efficients. The Car-
penter

penter rayseth not his frame without
tooles, nor the Deuill his woork without instrumentes : were not Players
the meane, to make these assemblyes,
such multitudes wold hardly be drawne
in so narowe roome. They seeke not
to hurte, but desire too please : they
haue purged their Comedyes of wanton speaches, yet the Corne whiche
they sell, is full of Cockle : and the
drinke that they drawe, ouercharged
with dregges. There is more in them
then we perceiue, the Deuill standes
at our elbowe when we see not, speaks,
when we heare him not, strikes when
wee feele not, and woundeth sore when
he raseth no skinne, nor rentes the
fleshe. In those thinges, that we least
mistrust, the greatest daunger dooth
often lurke. The Countryeman is
more affrayde of the Serpente that is
hid in the grasse, then the wilde beaste
that openly feeds vpon the mountains.
The Marriner is more indaungered by
priuie shelues, then knowen Rockes,
The Souldier is sooner killed with a
little

little Bullet, then a longe Swoorde;
There is more perill in close Fisto-
loes, then outwarde sores; in secret am-
bushe, then maine battels; in vndermi-
ning, then playne assaulting; in friends
then foes; in ciuill discorde, then for-
raine warres. Small are the abuses,
and sleight are the faultes, that nowe in
Theaters escape the Poets pen: But
tal Cedars, from little graynes shoote
high: great Okes, from slender rootes
spread wide: Large streames, from
narrowe springes runne farre: One
little sparke, fyers a whole Citie: One
dramme of Eleborus ransackes eue-
uery vaine: The Fish Remora hath a
small body, and greate force too staye
shippes against winde and tide: Ichneumon a litle worme, ouercomes the
Elephant: The Uiper slayes the Bul:
The Weesell the Cockatrice: And
the weakest Waspe, stingeth the stoutest manne of warre. The height of
Heauen, is taken by the staffe: The
bottome of the Sea, sounded with lead:
The farthest coast, discouered by Compasse:

passe: the secretes of nature, searched
by witte: the Anatomy of man, set out
by experience: But the abuses of plaies
cannot be showen, because they passe
the degrees of the instrument, reach of
the Plummet, sight of the minde, and
for trial are neuer brought to the touch-
stone. Therefore he that will auoyde the
open shame of prpuy sinne, the common
plague of priuate offences, the greate
wracks of little Rocks: the sure disease
of vncertaine causes: must set hande to
the sterne, and eye to his steppes, to
shunne the occasion as neere as he can:
neither running to bushes for renting
his clothes, nor rent his clothes for im-
paring his thrift; nor walke vpon Yse,
for taking a fall, nor take a fall for bru-
sing him selfe; nor goe too Theaters
for beeing allured, nor once bee allured
for feare of abuse.

Bunduica a notable woman and a
Queene of Englande, that tyme that
Nero was Emperour of Rome, hauing some of the Romans in garrison
heere against her, in an Oration which

she made to her subiects, seemed vtter-
ly to contemne their force, and laugh at
their folly. For shee accounted them
vnwoorthy the name of men, or title of
Souldiers, because they were smoothly
appareled, soft lodged, daintely feasted,
bathed in warme waters, rubbed with
sweet oyntments, strewd with fine poul-
ders, wine swillers, singers, Dauncers,
and Players.   God hath now blessed
England with a Queene, in vertue excellent, in power mightie, in glorye re-
nowmed, in gouernmnente politike, in
possession rich, breaking her foes with
the bent of her brow, ruling her subiects
with shaking her hand, remouing debate by diligent foresight', filling her
chests with the fruites of peace, mini-
string iustice by order of law, reforming
abuses with great regarde : & bearing
her sword so euen, that neither the poore
are trod vnder foote, nor the rich suffred
to loke too hye, nor Rome, nor France,
nor Tyrant, nor Turke, dare for their
liues too enter the List.   But wee vn-
worthy seruants of so milb a Distresse,
                              vnnatural

The Queenes
Maiestie.

vnnatural childzen of so good a mother,
vnthākful subiects of so louing a pzince,
wound her royall hart with abusing her
lenitie, and stir Iupiter to anger to send
vs a Stroke that shal deuoure vs. How
often hath her Maiestie with the graue
aduise of her honozable Councell, sette
downe the limits of apparell to euery
degree, and howsoone againe hath the
pzide of our harts ouerflowē the chanel?
How many times hath accesse to Theaters beene restrapned, and how boldly
againe haue we reentred? Ouerlashing
in apparel is so common a fault, that the
very hyerlings of some of our Players, Players men.
which stand at reuersion of vi.s, by the
weeke, iet vnder Gentlemens noses in
sutes of silke, exercising themselues too
pzating on the stage, & commō scoffing
when they come abzode, wherethey look
askāce ouer the shoulder of euery man,
of whom the sunday befoze they begged
an almes, I speake not this, as though
euerye one that professeth the qualitie
so abusedhim selfe, foz it is weli knowen, that some of them are sober
                              discrete

discreete, properly learned honest hou-
sholders and Citizens well thought on
amonge their neighbours at home ,
though the pryde of their shadowes (I
meane those hangebyes whome they
succour with stipend) cause them to bee
somewhat il talked of abroade. And as
some of the Players are farre from a-
buse: so some of their Playes are without rebuke: which are as easily remem-

bred as quickly reckoned . The twoo
prose Bookes plaied at the Belsauage,
where you shall finde neuer a woorde
without wit, neuer a line without pith,

neuer a letter placed in baine. The Iew
& Ptolome, showne at the Bull, the one
representing the greedinesse of worldly
chusers, and bloody mindes of Vsurers:
The other very liuely discrybing howe
seditious estates, with their owne deuises, false friendes, with their owne
swoordes, & rebellious comons in their
owne snares are ouerthrowne: neither
with Amorous gestrye wounding the
eye: nor with slouenly talke hurting the
eares of the chast hearers, The Blacke
Smiths

Smiths daughter, & Catilins conspira-
cies vsually brought in to the Theater:
The firste contayning the trechery of
Turkes, the honourable bountye of a
noble minde, & the shining of vertue in
distresse: The last, bicause it is knowen
too be a Pig of myne owne Sowe, I
will speake the lesse of it; onely giuing
you to vnderstand, that the whole marke
which I shot at in that woorke, was too
showe the rewarde of traytors in Cati-
lin, and the necessary gouernment of
learned men; in the person of Cicero,
which forsees euery dager that is likely to happen, and forstalles it continual-
ly ere it take effect. Therfore I giue
these Playes the commendation, that
Maximus Tyrius gaue too Homers
woorks: καλὰ ἃ μὲὼ γὸ τὰ Ομήρȣ ἐπικͬ
ἑπῶν τὰ κάλλιϛα, κͬ φανώϳατα κͬ ἅϛ-
δϳαι μούϛις πρέπονͳα ἀ᷁λα ὸ πᾶσι
καλὰ ὁ ͷͼ ἀικαλά.

¶ These Playes are good playes and
sweete playes, and of al playes the best
playes and most to be liked, woorthy to
bee soung of the Muses, or set out with
the

the cunning of Roscius himself, yet are they not fit for euery mans dyet: neither ought they commonly to bee shewen.

Players are not to be made common.

Now if any man aske me why my selfe haue penned Comedyes in time paste, & inueigh so egerly against them here, let him knowe that Semel insaniuimus omnes: I haue sinned, and am sorry for my fault: hee runnes farre that neuer turnes, better late then neuer. I gaue my self to that exercise in hope to thriue but I burnt one candle to seek another, and lost bothe my time and my trauell, when I had doone.

Thus sith I haue in my voyage suffred wrack with Vlisses, and wringing wet scambled with life to the shore, stãd from mee Nausicaä with all thy traine, till I wipe the blot from my forhead, and with sweet springs wash away the salt froath that cleaues too my soule.

Meane time if Players bee called to accounte for the abuses that growe by their assemblyes, I would not haue them to answere, as Pilades did for the Theaters of Rome, when they were

com‧

complayned on, and Augustus waxed *Dion in vita Augusti.*
angry: This resort O Cæsar is good for
thee, for heere we keepe thousandes
of idle heds occupyed, which else per-
aduéture would brue some mischiefe.
A fit Cloude to couer their abuse, & not
vnlike to the starting hole that Lucini-
us found, who like a greedy surueiour,
beeing sente into Fraunce to gouerne
the Countrie, robbed them and spoyled
them of all their Treasure with vntrea-
sonable taskes: et the last when his cru-
eltie was so loudely cryed out on, that
euery man hearde it; and all his pac- *Players com-pared to Lu-cinius.*
king did sauour so strõg, that Augustus
smelt it; be brought the good Emperour into his house, slapped him in the
mouth with a smoth lye, and tolde him
that for his sake & the safetie of Rome,
hee gathered those riches, the better to
impouerish the Countrie for rysing in
Armes, and so holde the poore French-
mennes Noses to the Grindstone for
euer after.

A bad excuse is better, they say
then none at all. Hee, because the
French

Frenchmē paid tribute euery moneth,
into xiiii. Moneths deuided the yeere:
These because they are allowed to play
euery Sunday, make iiii. or v. Sun-
dayes at least euery weeke, and all that
is doone is good for Augustus, to busy
the wittes of his people, for runuing a
woolgathering, and emptie their pur-
ses for thriuing to fast.   Though Lu-
cinius had the cast to playster vppe his
credite with the losse of his money : I
trust that they which haue the swoorde
in their hands among vs to pare away
this putryfied flesh, are sharper sighted,
and will not so easily be deluded.

Epist. 12. *ad
Lambertum.*

Marcus Aurelius sayth, That players falling from iuste labour to vniuste
idlenesse, doe make more trewandes,
and ill husvands, then if open Schooles
of vnthrifts & Vagabounds were kept.
Who soeuer readeth his Epistle too
Lambert the gouernor of Hellespont,
when Players were banished, shall find
more against them in plainer tearmes,
then I willl vtter.

This haue I set downe of the abuses
of

of Poets, Pypers, and Players which bringe vs too pleasure, slouth, sleepe, sinne, and without repentaunce to death and the Deuill: which I haue not confirmed by authoritie of the Scriptures, because they are not able to stand vppe in the sighte of God: and sithens they dare not abide the field, where the word of God dooth bidde them battayle, but runne to Antiquityes (though nothing be more ancient then holy Scriptures) I haue giuē them a volley of prophane writers to beginne the skirmishe, and doone my indeuour to beate them from their holdes with their owne weapons. The Patient that will be cured, of his owne accorde, must seeke the meane: if euery man desire to saue one, and drawe his owne feete from Theaters, it shall preuayle as much against these abuses, as Homers Moly against Witchcraft, or Plynies Peristerion against the byting of Dogges.

Scriptures too hoate for Players.

God hath armed euery creature against his enemie: The Lyon with pawes, the Bul with hornes, the Bore

D.   with

with tuskes, the Vulture with tallents, Hartes, Hindes, Hares, and such like, with swiftnes of feete, because they are fearefull, euery one of them putting his gift in practise; But man which is Lord of the whole earth, for whose seruice herbes, trees, rootes, plants, fish, foule & beasts of the fielde were first made, is far worse then the brute beasts: for they endewed but with sence, doe Appetere salutaria, & declinare noxia, seeke that which helpes them, and forsake that which hurtes them.

Man is enriched with reason and knowledge: with knowledge, to serue his maker and gouerne himselfe; with reason to distinguish good and il, I chose the best, neither referring the one to the glory of God, nor vsing the other to his owne profite. Fire and Ayre mount vpwards, Earth and Water sinke downe, & euery insensible body else, neuer rests, til it bring it self to his owne home. But we which haue both sense, reason, wit, and vnderstading, are euer ouerlasting, passing our boundes, going beyonde our

Corpora natura-
li a ad locum mo-
uentur, & in su-
is sedibus acqui-
escunt.

our limites, neuer keeping our selues within compasse, nor once loking after the place from whence we came, and whither we muste in spighte of our hartes.

Man vnmindful of his ende.

Aristotle thinketh that in greate windes, the Bees carry little stones in their mouthes too peyse their bodyes, leaft they bee carryed away, or kepte from their Hiues, vnto which they desire to returne with the fruites of their labour. The Crane is said to rest vpon one leg, and holding vp the other, keepe a Pebble in her clawe, which as sone as the senses are bound by approch of sleepe, falles to the ground, & with the noise of the knock against the Earth, makes her awake, whereby shee is euer redy to preuent her enemies. Geese are foolish birdes, yet whẽ they flye ouer the mount Taurus, they shew greate wisedome in their own defence: for they stop their pipes full of grauel to auoide gagling, & so by silence escape thẽ Eagles. Woodcocks, though they lack witte to

Hi. Animal.

D.2. same

saue them selues, yet they want not will to auoyde hurte, when they thrust theyr heades in a Bushe, and thinke their bodyes out of daunger. But wee which are so brittle, that we breake with euery sillop; so weake, that wee are drawne with euery threade; so light, that wee are blowen away with euery blaste; so vnsteady, that we slip in euery ground; neither peyse our bodyes againste the winde, nor stand vppon one legge, for sleeping too much: nor close vppe our lippes for betraping our selues, nor vse any witte, to garde our owne persons, nor shewe our selues willing too shunne our owne harmes, running most greedily to those places, where we are soonest ouerthrowne.

I cannot lyken our affection better than to an Arrowe, which getting lybertie, with winges is carryed beyonde our reach; kepte in the Quiuer, it is still at commaundement: Or to a Dogge, let him slippe, he is straight out of sight, holde him in the Lease, bee neuer stirres: Or to a Colte, giue him

the

the brídle, he flínges aboute; raíne hím
hard, & you may rule hím: Oꝛ to a ſhip,
hoyſt the ſayles it runnes on head; let
fall the Ancour, all is well: Oꝛ to
Pandoraes boꝛe, líſt vppe the líдde, out
flyes the Deuíll; ſhut it vp faſt, it cannot hurt vs.

Let vs but ſhut vppe our eares to
Poets, Pypers and Players, pull our
feete back from reſoꝛt to Theaters, and
turne away our eyes from beholdíng
of vanítíe, the greateſt ſtoꝛme of abuſe
wíll be ouerblowen, and a fayꝛe path
troдen to amendment of lífe. Were not
we ſo foolíſh to taſte euery дrugge, and
buy euery trífle, Players would ſhut in
theír ſhoppes, and carry theír traſhe to
ſome other Countríe.

Themiſtocles in ſetting a peece of
hís ground to ſale, among all the com-
modytíes whíche were reckoned vppe,
ſtraightly charged the Cryer to pꝛoclaíme thís, that hee whích bought ít,
ſhould haue a good neíghbour. If Players can pꝛomíſe in wooꝛдes, and per-
foꝛme ít in деедes, pꝛoclaíme ít in theír
D.3.   Billes₂

Billes, and make it good in Theaters,
that there is nothing there noysome too
the body, no2 hurtfull to the soule: and
that euerye one which comes to buye
their Iestes, shall haue an honest neigh-
bour, tagge and ragge, cutte and longe
taple, goe thither and spare not, otherwise I aduise you to keepe you thence,
my selfe will beginne too leade the
daunce.

I make iuste reckoning to bee helde
fo2 a Stoike, in dealing so hardely with
these people: but all the Keyes hang not
at one mans girdle, neither doe these o-
pen the lockes to all abuses. There are
other which haue a share with them in
their Schooles, therefore ought they to
daunce the same Rounde: and bee par-
takers together of the same rebuke:
Fencers, Dycers, Dauncers, Tum-
bles, Carders, and Bowlers.

Dauncers and Tumblers, because
they are dumbe Players, and I haue
glaunced at them by the way, shail bee
let passe with this clause; that they gather no assemblyes, and goe not beyond
the

Dauncers and Tumblers.

the precincts whiche Peter Martyr in his commentaryes vppon the Judges hath set them downe: That is, if they will exercise those qualpties, to doe it priutlye, for the health and agilitie of the body, referring all to the glorye of God.

Dicers and Carders because their abuses are as commonly cryed out on, as vsually shewen, haue no neede of a needelesse discourse, for euery manne seeth them, and they stinke almoste in euery mans nose. Common Bowling Allyes, are priuy Mothes, that eate vppe the credite of many idle Citizens : whose gaynes at home, are not able too weighe downe theyr losses abroade, whose Shoppes are so farre from maintaining their play, that their Wiues and Children cry out for bread, and go to bedde supperlesse ofte in the yeere.

I woulde reade you a Lecture of these abuses, but my Schoole so increaseth, that I cannot touch all, nor stand to

amplifie

ample euery poynte : one worde of
Fencing, and so a Conge to all kinde
of Playes. The knowledge in weapons may bee gathered to be necessary
in a common wealth, by the Senators
of Rome, who in the time of Catilins
conspyracyes, caused Schooles of Defence to be erected in Capua, that teaching the people howe to warde, and
how to locke, howe to thrust, and how
to strike, they might the more safelye
coape with their enemies. As the Arte
of Logique was firste sette downe for
a rule, by which wee mighte Confir-
mare nostra, & refutare aliena, confirme our owne reasons, and confute the
allegations of our aduersaryes, the end
beeing trueth, which once fished out by
the harde encounter of eithers Argu-
mentes, like fyer by the knocking of
flintes togither, bothe partes shoulde
be satisfyed and striue no more. And I
iudge that the crafte of Defence was
firste deuised to saue our selues harme-
lesse, and holde our enemies still at ad-
uaun-

Fencers.

Saluſt.

vauntage, the ende beeing right, which once throughly tryed out, at handye stroakes, neither hee that offered iniurie shoulde haue his will, nor hee that was threatened, take any hurte, but bothe be contented and shake handes. Those dayes are now chaunged, the skil of Logicians, is exercysed in caueling, the cunning of Fencers applied to quarrelling: they, thinke themselues no Schollers, if they bee not able to finde out a knotte in euery rushe; these, no men, if for stirring of a strawe, they prooue not their valure vppon some boodyes fleshe. Euery Duns will bee a Carper, euery Dick Swash a common Cutter. But as they bake, many times so they brue: Selfe doe, selfe haue, they whette their Swoordes against themselues, pull the house on their owne heds, returne home by weeping Crosse, and fewe of them come to an honest ende. For the same water that driues the Mill, decayeth it. The woode is eaten by the worme, that breeds within it: The goodnesse of a

D 5.   knife

knife cuts the owners finger. The Adders death, is her own broode, the Fencers scath, his own knowledg. Whether
their harts be hardened, which vse that
exercise, or God giue them ouer I know
not well: I haue reade of none good that
practised it muche.   Commodus the
Emperour, so delighted in it, that often
times hee slewe one or other at home, to
keepe his fingers in vre.   And one day
hee gathered all the sicke, lame, and
impotent people of Rome into one
place, where hee hamprd their feete
with straunge deuises, gaue them softe
spunges in their hands, to throw at him
for stones, & with a greate clubbe knat-
ched them all on the hed, as they had bin
Giauntes.   Epaminondas a famous
Captaine, sore hurte in a battaile, and
carryed out of the fielde, halfe deade :
When tydinges was broughte him
that his Souldiers gotte the day, asked
presently, what became of his Buckler: whereby it appeareth, that hee loued his weapons, but I finde it not sayd
that

Commodus a Fencer and ex-ercised in mur-der.

Epaminondas minde on his Buckler.

that he was a Fencer. Therfore I may
liken them which woulde not haue men
sent to war til they are taught fencinge,
to those superstitious wisemen, whiche
would not take vppon them to burye the
bodyes of their friends, before they had
beene cast vnto wilde beastes. Fencing
is growne to such abuse, that I may wel
compare the Scholers of this Schoole
to them that prouide Staues for their
owne shoulders; that foster Snakes, in
their owne bosoms; that trust Wolues,
to garde theyr Sheepe; And to the men
of Hyrcania, that keepe Mastiffes, to
woorye them selues . Thougbe I
speake this too the shame of common
Fencers, I goe not aboute the bushe
with Souldiers, Homer calleth them ^{Souldiers.}
the Sonnes of Iupiter, the Images
of G O D, and the very sheepeheards
of the people: beeing the Sonnes of
Iupiter, they are bountifull too the
meeke; and thunder out plagues to the
proude in heart: beeing the Images of
G O D, they are the Welspringes
                                   of

of Iustice which giueth to euery man his owne; beeing accoumpted the shepe-heards of the people, they fight with the Woolfe for the safette of their flock and keepe of the enimie for the wealth of their Countrie.   How full are Poets works of Bucklers, Battails, Lances, Dartes, Bowes, Quiuers, Speares, Iauelins, Swoordes, slaughters, Run-ners Wrestlers, Chariots, Horse, and men at armes? Agamemnon beyonde the name of a King hath this title, that he was a Souldier. Menelaus, because he loued his Kercher better then a Bur-gonet, a softe bed then a hard fielde, the founde of Instrumentes then neighing of Steedes, a fayre stable then a foule way, is let slippe without prayse. If Lycurgus before hee make lawes too Sparta, take counsel of Apollo, whether it were good for him to teach the peo-ple thrift and husbandry, he shalbe char-ged to leaue those precepts to the white liuered Hylotes.   The Spartans are all steele, fashioned out of tougher mettall,

free

free in minde, valiaunt in hart, seruile to
none, accustoming their flesh to stripes,
their boddes to labour, their feete to
hunting, their handes to fighting. In
Crete, Scythia, Persia, Thracia, all the
Lawes tended to the maintenance of
Martiall disciplyne. Among the Scythians no man was permitted to drink
of their festiuall Cuppe, which had not
manfully killed an enemie in fight. I
coulde wishe it in England, that there
were greater preferment for the valiant
Spartanes, then the sottishe Hylotes:
That our Lawes were directed to re-
warding of those, whose liues are the
firste, that must be hazarded to mayntaine the lybertie of the Lawes. The
gentlemen of Carthage, were not allow
ed too weare, any moe linkes in their
chaynes, then they had seene battayles.
If our Gallantes of Englande might
carry no more linkes in their Chaynes
nor ringgs on their fingers, then they
haue fought feeldes, their necks shoulo
not bee very often wreathed in Golde,
nor their handes embrodered with pre-
ciouß

cious stones. If none but they might be suffered to drinke out of plate, that haue in skirmish slain one of her maiesties enemyes, many thousands shoulde bring earthen pots to the table. Let vs learne by other mens harmes too looke to our selues, When the Ægyptians were most busy in their husbandry, the Scythians ouerran them: when the Assyrians were looking to their thrift, the Persians wer in armes & ouercam thē: when the Troians thoughte them selues safest, the Greekes were neerest: when Rome was a sleepe, the French men gaue a sharpe assaulte too the Capitoll: when the Iewes were idle, their walles were rased, & the Romans entred: when the Chaldees were sporting, Babylon was sacked: when the senators were quiet, no garrisons in Italy, & Pōpey frō home, wicked Catiline began his mischeuous enterprise. We are like those vnthankfull people, which puffed vp with prosperity forget the good turnes they receiued in aduersitie. The patient feeds his Phisition wt gold in time of sicknesse, & when he

be is wel, scarcely affoords him a cup of
water. Some there are that make gods
of soldiers in open warrs, & trusse them
vp like dogs in the time of peace. Take
heed of the foresaid nightcap, I meene
those schoolemen, that cry out vpō Mars
calling him the bloody God, the angry
God, the furious god, the mad God, πο-
λυδ'ακρυν the tearethirsty God. These
are but castes of their office & woordes of
course. That is a vain brag & a false allarme, that Tullie giues to soldiers.

Cedant arma togæ, cōcedat laurea lingue.
Let gunns to gouns, & bucklers yeeld to
bookes. If the enemy beseege vs, cut off
our victuals, preuent forrain aide, girt in
the city, & bring the Rāme to ȳ walles,
it is not Ciceroes tongue that cā peerce
their armour to woūd the body, nor Ar-
chimedes prickes, & lines, & circles, &
triangles, & Rhombus, & risseraffe, that
hath any force to driue them backe.
Whilst the one chats, his throte is cut;
whilest the other syttes drawing
Mathematicall fictions, the enimie
standes with a swoorde at his breast.
                                    He

He that talketh much, and doth litle, is like vnto him that sailes with a side winde, and is borne with the tide to a wrong shore. If they meane to doe any good indeed, bid them followe Demosthenes, and ioyne with Phocion: when they haue giuen vs good counsell in wordes, make much of Souldiers, that are redy to execute þ same with swordes. Bee not carelesse, Plough with weapons by your sides, studye with a booke in one hande, a darte in the other: enioy peace, with prouision for war: when you haue lefte the sandes behinde you, looke wel to the rocks that lye before you: Let not the ouercōming one Tempest make you secure, but haue an eye to the cloude that comes from the South, and threatenethraine: the least ouersight in dangerous Seas may cast you awaye, the least discontinuaunce of Martial exercise giue you the foyle. When Achilles loytered in his tent, giuing eare too Musick, his souldiers were bidde to a hot breakefast. Hannibals power receiues

reiued more hurte in one dayes eale at
Capua, then in al the conflicts they had
at Cannas. It were not good for vs too
flatter oure selues with thefe golden
dayes: highe floodes haue lowe Ebbes:
hotte Feuers, coulde Crampes: Long
dayes shorte nightec; Drie Summers
moyst VVinters: There was neuer fort
so strõg, but it might be battered, neuer
grcũd so fruitful, but it might be barrẽ:
neuer coũtrie so populous, but it might
te wast: neuer Monarch so mighty; but
he might be weakened : neuer Realme
so large, but it might be lessened: neuer
kingdom so florishing, but it might bee
decayed. Scipio before hee leuied his
force too the walles of Carhage, gaue
his souldiers the print of the Citie in a
cake to bee deuoured: our enimies with
Scipio , haue already eaten vs with
bread, & licked vp our blood in a cup of
wine. They do but tarry the tide: watch
opportunitie, and wayte for the reckoning, that with the shot of our liues,
shoulde paye for all. But that G O D,
that neither slumbreth nor sleepeth , for
the loue of Israel, that stretcheth out
E   his

his armes from moꝛning to euening to
couer his childꝛen, (as the Hen doth her
chicken with the shadow of her wings)
with the bꝛeath of his mouth shall ouer-
thꝛow them, with their own snares shall
ouertake them, & hang them vp by the
haire of their owne deuises. Notwithstanding it behooueth vs in the meane
season, not to stick in the myꝛe, and gape
foꝛ succour, without vsing some oꝛdina-
ry way our selues : oꝛ to lye wallowing
like Lubbers in the Ship of the common wealth, crying Loꝛd, Loꝛd, when
wee see the vessel toyle, but ioyntly laye
out handes and heades, and helpes together, to auoyd the danger, & saue that,
which must be the suretie of vs all. Foꝛ
as to the body, there are many mēbers,
seruing to seuerall vses, the eye to see,
the eare to heare, the nose to smell, the
tongue to taste, the hande to touch, the
feete to beare the whole burden of the
rest, and euery one dischargeth his duetie without grudging; so shoulde the
whole body of the common wealth con-
sist of fellow laboꝛers, all generally seruing one head, & particularly following
their

their trade, without repining. From the
head to the foote, from the top to the toe,
there should nothing be vaine, no body
idle. Iupiter himself shall stand for exã-
ple, who is euer in woork, still moouing
& turning about the heauens, if he shuld
pull his hand from the frame, it were
impossible for the world to indure. All
would be day, or al night; All spring, or
all Autume; all Summer, or all winter;
All heate or all colde; all moysture, or al
drought; No time to til, no time to sow,
no time to plant, no time to reape, the
earth barren, the riuers stopt, the Seas
stayde, the seasons chaunged, and the
whole course of nature ouerthrowe. The
meane must labor to serue the mightie,
the mightie must studye to defende the
meane. The subiects must sweat in obedience to their Prince; the Prince must
haue a care ouer his poore vassals. If it
be the dutie of euery man in a common
wealth, one way or other to bestirre his
stumpes, I cãnot but blame those lither
cõtemplators very much, which sit con-
cluding of Sillogismes in a corner,
which in a close study in the Uniuersity

Loyterers.

coope themselues vp fortie yeres togither studying all thinges, and professe
nothing. The Bell is knowen by his
sounde, the Byrde by her voyce, the
Lyon by his rore, the Tree by the
fruite, a man by his woorkes. To
continue so long without moouing, to
reade so much without teaching, what
differeth it from a dumbe Picture, or a
deade body? No man is borne to seeke
priuate profite: parte for his countrie,
parte for his friendes, parte for himselfe. The foole that comes into a
fayre Garden, likes the beawtie of
flowers, and stickes them in his Cap:
the Phisition considereth their nature,
and puttes them in the potte: in the one
they wither without profite; in the other
they serue to the health of the bodie: He
that readeth good writers, and pickes
out their flowers for his owne nose, is
lyke a foole; hee that preferreth their
vertue before their sweet smel is a good
Phisition. When Anacharsis traueled
ouer all Greece, to seek out wise men,
hee sounde none in Athens, though no
doubt, there were many good scholers
there

there, But comming to Chenas a blind village, in comparison of Athens a Paltockes Inne; he found one Miso, well gouerning his house, looking to his grounde, instructing his children, teaching his family, making of marriages among his acquayntance, exhorting his neighbours to loue, & friendeship, & preaching in life, who, the Philosopher for his scarcitie of woordes, plenty of woorkes, accompted the onelye wise man that euer he saw. I speak not this to preferr Botley before Oxeford, a cottage of clownes, before a Colledge of Muses; Pans pipe, before Apollos harp. But to shew you that poore Miso can reade you such a lecture of Philosophie, as Aristotle neuer dreamed on. You must not thruste your heades in a tubbe, & say, *Bene vixit, qui bene latuit:* Hee hath liued well, that hath loitred well: standing streames geather filth; flowing riuers, are euer sweet. Come foorth with your sicles, the Haruest is greate, the laborers few; pul vp the sluices, let out your springs, geue vs drink of your water, light of your torches, &

E 3   season

seafon vs a little with the Salt of your
knowledge. Let Phænix and Achilles,
Demofthenes & Phocion, 'Pericles &
Cimon, Lælius & Scipio, Nigidius and
Cicero, the word and the sword be knit
togither. Set your talents a worke, lay
not vp your tresure for takingtruff, teach
earely & late, in time & out of time, sing
with the swan, to the last houre. Folowe
the dauncing Chaplens of Gradiuus
Mars, which chaunt the praises of their
god with voyces, and treade out the
time to their feete. Play the good captaines, exhort your souldiers with your
tonges to fight, & bring the first ladder
to the wall your selues. Sound like bels,
and shine like Lanternes; Thunder in
words, and glister in workes; so shall you
please God, profite your country, honor
your prince, discharge your duetie, giue
vp a good account of your stewardship,
and leaue no sinne vntouched, do abuse
vnrebuked, no fauk vnpunished. Sundry are the abuses aswell of Vniuersi-
ties as of other places, but they are
such as neither become me to touch, nor
query idle yed to vnderstand. The Thu-
rines

Carpers.

rines made a Lawe that no common
findefault should meddle with any abuse
but Adulterie. Pythagoras bounde
all his Schollers to fiue yeeres silence,
that assoone as euer they crept from the
shel, they might not aspire to the house
top. It is not good for euery man too
trauell to Corinth, nor lawfull for all
to talke what they liste, or write what
they please, least their tongues run before their wites, or their pennes make
hauock of their Paper. And so wading
too farre in other mens manners, whilst
they fill their Bookes with other mens
faultes, they make their volumes no
better then an Apothecaries Shop, of
pestilent Drugges; a quackesaluers
Budget of filthy receites; and a huge
Chaos of foule disorder. Cookes did
neuer long more for great markets, nor
Fishers for large Ponds, nor greedy
Dogges for store of game, nor soaring
hawkes for plentie of fowle, then Carpers doe nowe for coppe of abuses,
that they might euer be snarling, and
haue some Flyes or other in the way to
snatch at. As I woulde that offences

should

should not be hid, for going vnpunished, nor escape thout scourge for ill example. So I wish that euery rebuker shoulde place a hatch before the doore; keep his quil twin compas, He that holds not him self contented with the light of the Sun but liftes vp his eyes to measure the bignesse, is made blinde; he that bites euery weed to search out his nature, may light vpon poyson, and so kill him selfe: he that loues to be sifting of euery cloude, may be strooke with a thunder bolte, if it chaunce to rent; & he that ta keth vpon him to shew men their faultes, may wound his owne credite, if he goe too farre. We are not angry with the Clarke of the market, if he come to our stall, and reprooue our balllance when they are faultie, or forfaite our weightes, when they are false: neuerthelesse, if he presume to enter our house, and rig euery corner, searching woze then belongs to his office: we lay holde on his locks, turne him away with his backe full of stripes, and his hands loden with his owne amendes. Therefore I will con tent my selfe to shew you no moze abu
ses

res in my Schoole, then my selfe haue
seene, nor so many by hundreds, as I
haue heard off. Lyons folde vp their
nailes, when they are in their dennes for
wearing them in the earth and neede
not : Eagles draw in their tallants as
they sit in their nestes, for blunting the
there amonge drosse: And I will caste
Ancor in these abuses, rest my Barke in
the simple roade, for grating my wits
vpon needelesse shelues, And because I
accuse other for treading awry, which
since I was borne neuer went right; because I finde so many faultes abroade,
which haue at home more spots in my
body then the Leopard; more staines on
my coate then the wicked Nessus; more
holes in my life then the open Siue ;
more sinnes in my soule than heares on
my bed; If I haue beene tedious in my
Lecture, or your selues be weary of
your lessou, harken no longer
for the Clock, shut vp
the Schoole, and
get you home.

FINIS.

To the right honorable
Sir Richard Pipe, Knight, Lorde
Maior of the Citie of London, and the
right worshipful his brethren, con-
tinuance of health and mainte-
nance of ciuil gouernment.

ERICLES was
woont (Right ho-
nourable and wor-
shipful) as oft as he
put on his robes, to
preach thus vnto
himselfe : Consider
wel *Pericles*, what thou doest, thou
commaundest free men, the Greekes
obey thee, & thou gouernest the Citizens of Athens. If you say not so
much to your selues, the gownes that
you weare, as the cognisances of authoritie; and the sword which is cari-
ed before you, as the instrument of
iustice; are of sufficient force to pur
you in mind, that you are the masters
of free men, that you gouerne the
worshipfull Citizens of London, and
that you are the very Stewards of her
Maiestie

Maieſtie within your liberties. Therfore ſith by mine owne experience I
haue erected a Schoole of thoſe a-
buſes, which I haue ſeene in *London*,
I preſume the more vpon your pardon, at the ende of my Phamphlet
to preſent a fewe lynes to your honourable reading.

Auguſtus the good Emperour of
Rome, was neuer angry with accuſers
becauſe hee thought it neceſſarye
(where many abuſes flouriſh) for e-
uery man freely to ſpeake his minde.
And I hope that *Auguſtus* (I meane
ſuch as are in authoritie) will beare
with me, becauſe I touch that which
is needefull to bee ſhewen. Wherein
I goe not about to inſtruct you howe
to rule, but to warne you what danger hangs ouer your heads, that you
may auoyde it.

The Byrde *Trochilus* with craſhing
of her bil awakes the *Crocodile*, and
deliuereth her from her enemyes,
that are readye too charge her in
deade, ſleepe, A little fiſhe, ſwimmeth
con-

continnally before the great Whale,
to shewe him the shelues, that he run
not a ground: The Elephants, when
any of their kinde are fallen into the
pittes, that are made to catch them,
thrust in stones and earth to recouer
them: When the Lyon is caught in
a trap, *Æsops* Mouse by nibling the
cordes sets him at libertie. It shall be
inough for me with *Trochilus* to haue
wagged my bil; with the little Fish to
haue gone before you; with the Elephants to haue shewed you the way
to helpe your selfe; and with *Æ-*
sops mouse to haue fretted the snares
with a byting tooth for your owne
safetie.

The *Thracians* when they must
passe ouer frosen streames, sende out
theyr Wolues, whiche laying their
eares to the yse, listen for noyse: If
they hear any thing, they gather that
it mooues; if it mooue, it is not congealed; If it be not congealed, it must
be liquide; If it be liquide, then will
it yeelde; and if it yeelde, it is not
                              good

good trusting it with the weight of
their bodyes, leste they sincke. The
worlde is so slippery, that you are often inforced to passe ouer Yse. Therfore I humbly beseech you to try farther, & trust lesse, not your Woolues,
but many of your Citizens haue al-
read sifted the daunger of your pas-
sage, and in sifting beene swallowed
to their discredite.

I would the abuses of my Schoole
were as wel knowen of you, to refor-
mation: as they are found out by o-
ther to their owne peril. But the fishe
Sepia can trouble the water to shun
the nettes, that are shot to catch her:
Torpedo hath craft inough at the first
touch to inchant the hooke, to con-
iure the line, to bewitch the rod, and
too benumme the handes of him
that angleth. Whether our Players
be the Spawnes of such fishes, I know
not wel, yet I am sure that how many
nets sooner they be layde to take thē,
or hoökes to choke them, they haue
Ynke in their bowels to darken the
                                    water

water, and fleights in their budgets, to dry vp the arme of euery Magi-strate. If their letters of commenda-tions were once ftayed, it were eafie for you to ouerthrowe them. *Agefi-laus* was greatly rebuked, becaufe in matters of iuftice, he inclined to his friends and became partiall. *Plutarch* condemneth this kinde of writinge, *Niciam, fi nihil admifit noxæ, exime ; Si quid admifit, mihi exime; omnino autem hominem noxæ exime* . If *Nicias* haue not offended, meddle not with him: If hee be guiltie, forgiue him for my fake, What foeuer you doe, I charge you acquite him. This inforceth Ma-giftrates like euill Poets to break the feete of their verfe, and finge out of tune, and with vnfkilful Carpenters, to vfe the Square and the compaffe, the Rule and the Quadrant, not to builde, but to ouerthrow.

Bona verba quæfo. Some fay that it is not good iefting with edge toles: The Athĕniĕns will mince *Phocion* as fmall as flefhe to the potte, if they

be

bemad: but kil *Demades* if they beé
sober: And I doubte not but the go-
uernours of *London* will vexe meé
for speaking my minde, when they
are out of their wittes, and banishe
their Players, when they are beste
aduised.

In the meane time it behooueth your Honour in your charge,
too play the Musition, streatch e-
uery string till hee breake, but sette
him in order. · Hee that will haue
the Lampe too burne cleere, must
aswell powre in Oyle to nourish thé
flame, as snuffe the Weeke, to in-
crease the light. If your Honour
desire too see the Citie well gouer-
ned, you must aswell sette to your
hand to thrust out abuses, as shewe
your selfe willing to haue all amen-
ded. · And (least I seeme one of
those idle Mates, which hauing nothing to buy at home, and lesse too
sell in the market abrode, stand at a
boothe, if it be but to gase; or wan-
ting worke in mine owne study, and
                              hauing

hauinge no wit to gouerne Cities, yet
busye my braynes with your honorable office) I wil heere ende, desi-
ring pardon for my faulte,
because I am rashe; &
redresse of abuses,
because they
ar naught.

Your Honors &c.
to commaunde.

Stephan Gosson.

P.

The

To the Gentlewomen Citizens of London, Flourishing dayes with regarde of Credite.

THE reuerence that I owe you Gentlewomen, because you are Citizens; & the pitie wherwith I tender your case, because you are weake; hath thrust out my hād, at the breaking vp of my Schoole, to write a few lines to your sweete selues. Not that I thinke you to bee rebuked, as idle huswiues, but commended and incouraged as vertuous Dames. The freest horse, at the whiske of a wand, girdes forwarde: The swiftest Hound, when he is hallowed, strippes forth: The kindest Mastiffe, when he is clapped on the backe, fighteth best: The stoutest Souldier, when the Trumpet sounds, strikes fiercest: The gallantest Runner, when the people showte, getteth grounde: and the perfectest liuers, when they are praysed, winne greatest credits.

I haue

I haue seene many of you whiche were
wont to sporte your selues at Theaters, whē
you perceiued the abuse of those places,
schoole your selues,& of your owne accorde
abhorre Playes. And sith you haue begun
to withdrawe your steppes,continew so stil,
if you be chary of your good name.For this
is generall,that they which shew thēselues.
openly, desire to bee seene.It is not a softe
shooe that healeth the Gowte; nor a golden
Ring that driueth away the Crampe;nor a
crown of Pearle that cureth the Megrim;
nor your sober countenance,that defendeth
your credite,nor your friends which accom-
pany your person,that excuse your folly:nor
your modestie at home,that couereth your
lightnesse,if you present your selues in open
Theaters.Thought is free:you can forbidd
no man,that vieweth you,to noute you,and
that nouteth you,to iudge you,for entring to
places of suspition. Wilde Coltes,when they
see their kinde begin to bray;& lusty bloads
at the showe of faire women, giue a wanton
sigh, or a wicked wishe. Blasing markes are
most shot at,glistring faces cheefly marked;
and what followeth? Looking eyes, haue ly-

king hartes, liking harts may burne in lust,
We walke in the Sun many times for pleasure, but our faces are tāned before we returne: though you go to theaters to se sport,
Cupid may catche you ere you departe.
The litle God houereth aboute you, & fan-
neth you with his wings to kindle fire: when
you are set as fixed whites, Desire draweth
his arrow to the head, & sticketh it oppe to
the fethers, and Fancy bestirreth him too
shed his poyson through euery vaine. If you
doe but listen to the voyce of the Fouler, or
ioyne lookes with an amorous Gazer, you
haue already made your selues assaultable,
& yelded your Cities to be sacked. A wanton eye is the darte of Cephalus, where it
leueleth, there it lighteth; & where it hitts,
it woundeth deepe. If you giue but a glance
to your beholders, you haue vayled the bón-
net in token of obedience : for the boulie is
falne ere the Ayre clap; the Bullet paste,
ere the Peece crack; the colde taken, ere the
body shiuer; and the match made, ere you
strike handes.

　　To auoyd this discommoditie, Cyrus refused to looke vppon Panthea, And Alex-
　　　　　　　　　　　　　　　　　ander

ander the great on Darius wife. The ficke
man that relisheth nothing, when hee seeth
some about him feede apace, and commend
the taste of those dishes which hee refused,
blames not the meate, but his owne disease:
And I feare you will say, that it is no ripe
iudgement, but a rawe humor in my selfe,
which makes me condemne the resorting to
Playes; because there come many thyther,
which in your opinion sucke no poyson, but
feede hartely without hurt; therefore I doe
very ill to reiect that which other like, and
complaine still of mine owne maladie.

In deede I must confesse there comes to
Playes of all sortes, old and young; it is hard
to say that all offend, yet I promise you, I wil
sweare for none. For the driest flax flameth
soonest; & the greenest wood smoketh most;
gray heads have greene thoughts; and young
slippes are olde twigges. Beware of those
places, which in sorrowe cheere you, and be-
guile you in mirth. You must not cut your
bodyes to your garmentes, but make your
gownes fit to the proportion of your bodyes;
nor fashiō your selues, to open spectacles, but
tye all your sportes to the good disposition of

a ver-

a vertuous minde. At Diceplay, euery one
wisheth to caste well; at Bowles euery one
craues to kisse the maister; at running eue-
ty one starteth to win the goale; At shoting
euery one striues to hit the marke; and will
not you in all your pastimes and recreations
seeke that which shall yeelde you most profite & greatest credite? I wil not say you are
made to toile, & I dare not graunt that you
should be idle. But if there be peace in your
houses, and plentie in your Coafers, let the
good precept of Xenophō be your exercise:
in all your ease and prosperitie, remember
God, that he may be mindefal of you, when
your heartes grone, And succour you still in
the time of neede. Be euer busied in godly
meditations: seeke not to passe ouer the gulf
with a tottering plank that wil deceiue you.
When we cast off our best clothies, we put on
ragges, when our good desires are once laide
aside, wantonwil begins to prick. Being pen-
siue at home, if you go to Theaters to driue
away fancies, it is as good Physike, as for
the ache of your head to knocke out your
braines; or when you are stung with a Wasp,
to rub the sore with a Nettle. When you

greened, passe the time with your neigh-
boures in sober conference, or if you
canne reade, let Bookes bee your comforte.
Doe not imitate those foolish Patientes,
which hauing sought all meanes of recoue-
ry & are neuer the neere, run vnto witch-
craft.If your greefe be such, that you may not
disclose it,& your sorrowe so great, that you
loth to vtter it, looke for no salue at Playes
or Theaters, lest that laboring to shun Silla,
you light on Charibdis;to forsake the depe,
you perish in sands; to warde a light stripe,
you take a deathes wound; and to leaue Phi-
sike, you flee to inchaunting. You neede not
goe abroade to bee tempted, you shall bee in-
tised at your owne windowes. The best coun-
cel that I can giue you, is to keepe home, &
shun all occasion of ill speech. The virgins
of Vesta were shut vp fast in stone walles to
the same end. You must keepe your sweete
faces from scorching in the Sun, chapping in
the winde, and warping with the weather,
which is best performed by staying within.
And if you perceiue your selues in any danger at your owne doores, either allured by
curtasie, or assaulted with Musike
wo

To the Gentlewomen

in the night ; Close vppe your eyes, stoppe
your eares, tye vp your tounges ; when they
speake, answeare not ; when they hallowe,
stoope not ; when they sighe, laugh at them ;
when they sue, scorne them ; Shunne their
company, neuer be seene where they resort ;
so shall you neither set them proppes when
they seeke to climbe; nor holde them the stir-
rope when they proffer to mount.

These are harde lessons whiche I teache
you ; neuerthelesse , drinke vppe the po-
tion, though it like not your tast , and you shal
be eased; resist not the Surgeon, though hee
strike in his knife, and you shall bee cured .
The Fig tree is sower, but it yeeldeth sweett
fruite : Thymus is bittter, but it giueth
Honny; my Schoole is tarte, but my counsell
is pleasant , if you imbrace it . Shortly I hope
to send ont the discourses of my Phyalo,
by whom (if I see you accept this)
I wil giue you one dish for
your own tooth.
Farewel.

Yours to serue at Vertues call,
Stephan Gosson.

Appendix

Title page from Huntington
61175, *STC* 12097.

THE
Shoole of Abuse,

Conteining a plesaunt in-
uectiue against Poets , Pipers,
Plaiers , Iesters, and such like
Caterpillers of a Comonwelth:

Setting vp the Flagge of Defiance to their
mischieuous exercise , & ouerthrow-
ing their Bulwarkes, by Prophane
Writers, Naturall reason, and
common experience:

A discourse as pleasaunt for
Gentlemen that fauour learning,as profitable for all that wyll
follow vertue.

By Stephan Gosson. Stud. Oxon.

Tuscul . 1

Mādare literis cogitationes, nec eas dispo-
nere,nec il'ustrare, nec delectatione a-
liqua allicere Lectorem, hominis est in-
temperanter abutentis , & otio , &
literis.

Printed at London,by Thomas
VVoodcocke. 1579.

A Reply to Gosson's
Schoole of Abuse

Thomas Lodge

Preface

This first extant work of Thomas Lodge, a brief reply to Gosson's Schoole of Abuse, *survives in two copies only (Heber [VIII, 4222]-Rodd-Malone-Bodleian, and Beauclerc-Nassau-Heber [II, 2334]-Britwell-Huntington), neither possessing a title, date, imprint, or attribution, although the latter bears an inscription in a contemporary hand at the head of A1: "Here bigineth Mr Lodges reply t[o] Stephen Gosson touchinge playes." There is no reason, with* STC *[1926] and Lowe-Arnott-Robinson, to declare the extant version defective; it would seem rather that the ill-printed and corrupt little tract was issued as it now appears— unaccompanied by preliminaries of any kind, and suppressed at or very shortly after its publication. For in his* Alarum against Usurers *(1584), Lodge gives this account: "About three yeres ago [sic], one* Stephen Gosson *published a booke, intituled* The School of Abuse, *in which having escaped in many and sundry occasions, I, as the occasion then fitted me, shapt him such an answere as beseemed*

3

his discourse; by which reason of the slenderness of the subject, (because it was in defence of plaies and play makers) the godly and reverent that had to deale in the cause, misliking it, forbad the publishing. . . ." Nonetheless Gosson, Lodge complains, *"comming by a private imperfect coppye, about two yeres since made a reply* [Playes Confuted in Five Actions, *1582],"* which impugned in slanderous detail the character and morals of his antagonist—perhaps the more galling in that Lodge was son of the former Lord Mayor of London, and Gosson's dedicatee none less than Sir Francis Walsingham, a figure who bulks large in the personal life of the former *(see C.J. Sisson, ed.,* Thomas Lodge and Other Elizabethans *[1933], esp. pp. 145ff.).*

A slightly modernized but superior edition of the untitled "Reply to Gosson," along with the Alarum against Usurers *was prepared by David Laing for the Shakespeare Society in 1853. E.K. Chambers' extract (*Elizabethan Stage, *IV, 206) is taken from Laing's text, although G.G. Smith's abridgment, in* Elizabethan Critical Essays *(1904), had gone back to the Bodleian original.*

The twenty-four-leaf pamphlet collates A-C^8, although Laing describes it as sixteen pages long *and Hazlitt as sixteen leaves. It is undated but surely [1579-80], and while the printer is not named, he is not improbably the most interesting Hugh Singleton.*[1] *For several characteristics of the "Reply" match up very closely with other work by Singleton in this immediate period: the one initial "P" closely resembles a set of initials known to be Singleton's, both in foliation, the double-line border, and the deteriorated condition; the style of signing (arabic numbers) is also characteristic, the font of the main text was certainly in his stock (cf. esp.* STC *25258.5) as were the distinctly unusual type ornaments which make up the terminal border, and the small superior page numbers; and these page numbers are laid out precisely as in the example just cited. If indeed Singleton printed this first extant work of Lodge in 1579-80, we have a remarkable group of texts and authors to associate with him at exactly this time. In 1579, again without identifying himself, Singleton had printed John Stubbs's* Discoverie of a Gaping Gulf, *one of the most notoriously daring political tracts of the whole reign, and not only was pardoned (while Stubbs lost his right hand), but soon after was*

[1] *Miss Katherine F. Pantzer of the Houghton Library is principally responsible for this suggestion and the evidence adduced below.*

PREFACE

made Printer to the City of London (see Duff, A
Century of the English Book Trade *[1905], p.
148)—leading one to wonder upon whose informa-
tion John Stubbs was apprehended. But also in
1579 Singleton produced the first book of a
schoolmate of Lodge's at Merchant Taylors' under
Mulcaster, Edmund Spenser's* Shepherd's Calendar.
*The evidence and its implications deserve further
investigation, but we may, in this intriguing coinci-
dence, find a pattern or grouping similar to the
celebrated complication of the Stratfordian printer
Richard Field, Shakespeare, Antonio Perez,* Love's
Labours Lost, *and the 1594* Pedaços de Historia.

Our reprint is of Bodleian Malone Add. 896.
STC *16663 [recording 0 only];* Britwell Handlist,
II, 601; Lowe-Arnott-Robinson 253.

January, 1973   A.F.

Rotogenes can know *Apelles* by his line though he se him not, and wise men can consider by the Penn the aucthoritie of the wꝛiter thoughe they know him not. the Rubie is discerned by his pale rednes, and who hath not hard that the Lyon is knowne by hys clawes. though *Æsopes* craftie crowe be neuer so deftlye decked, yet is his double dealing eselp desiphered: & though men neuer so perfectly pollish there wꝛytings with others sentences, yet the simple truth wil discouer the shadow of ther follies: and bestowing euery fether in the bodye of the right M. tourne out the naked dissembler into his owen cote, as a spectacle of follye to all those which can rightlye Iudge what imperfections be. There came to my hands lately a litle (woulde God a wittye) pamphelet, baring a fayꝛe face as though it were the scoole of a buse but being by me aduisedly wayed I fynd it the oftscome of imperfections, the wꝛiter fuller of woꝛdes then iudgement, the matter certaiuely as ridiculus as serius. asuredly his mother witte wꝛought this wonder, the child to dispꝛayse his father the dogg to byte his mayster foꝛ

A   his

t is dainty mozcell. but I se(with *Seneca*)ÿ
the wzong is to be suffered, since he dispzay-
seth, who dy. costome. hath left to speake
well. but I meane to be shozt: and teach the
Maister what he knoweth not, partly that
he may se his own follie, and partly that I
may discharge my promisse, both kinde me:
therefoze I would wish the good scholmay-
ster to ouer looke his abuses: againe with
me, so shall he se an ezzon of infirmities
which begin in his first prinsiple in the dis-
pzayse of poetry. And first let me familiarly
consider with this find faulte, what the learned haue alwayes esteemed of poetrie. Sene-
ta thoughe a stoike would haue a poeticall
sonne, and amongst the auncientest *Homer*
was no lesse accompted then *Humanus deus*:
what made *Alexander* I pray you esteeme of
him so much? why allotted he foz his wozke
so curious a closset? was ther no fitter vnder
pzop foz his pillow thē a simple pamphelet?
in all *Darius* cofers was there no Iewell so
costly? foz sooth I my thinks these two (the one
the father of Philosophers; the other the
cheftaine of chiualrie) were both deceiued
if all were as a *Gosson* would with them, yf
Poetry payut naughte but paltrie toyes in
verse, ↓ their studies tended to folishnesse,
and

and in all their indeuors they i id naught els
but *agendo nihil agere* . Lord howe *Virgils*
poore gnatt pricketh him , and how *Ouids*
fley byteth him , he can beare no bourde, he
hath raysed vp a new sect of serius stoikes,
that can abide naught but their owen shadowe, and alow nothing worthye, but what
they conceaue, Did you neuer reade (my o-
uer wittie frend) that vnder the persons of
beastes many abuses were dissiphered: haue
you not reason to wape? that whatsoeuer é-
ther *Virgil* did write of his gnatt, or *Ouid* of
his fley : was all couertly to declare abuse?
but you are (*homo literatus*) a man of the
letter litile sauoring of learning, your giddy
brain made you leaue your thrift, and your
abuses in London some part of your hone-
stie. You say that Poets are subtil, if so, you
haue learned that poynt of them , you can
well glose on a trifleling text. but you haue
dronke perhaps of *Lethe*, your gramer learning is out of your head, you forget your
Accidence, you remember not, that vnder the
person of *Æneas* in *Virgil* the practice of a
dilligent captaine is discribed vnder ÿ shadow of byrds, beastes and trees, the follies
of the world were disiphered, you know not,
that the creation is signified in the Image

A.2.   of

of *Prometheus*, the fall of pryde in the person
of *Narcissus*, these are topes because they sa
uor of wisedome which you want. Marke
what *Campanus* sayth, *Mira fabularum va-*
nitas sed quæ si introspiciantur videri possunt
non vanæ. The vanitie of tales is wonderful, yet if we aduisedly looke into them
they wil seme & proue wise. how wonderful
are the pithie poemes of *Cato*? the curious
comidies of *Plautus*? how brauely discoue-
reth *Terence* our imperfectiō in his *Eunuch*?
how neatly dissiphereth he *Danus*? how plea
sauntly paynteth he out *Gnatho*? whom if
we should seeke in our dayes, I suppose he
would not be farr from your parson. But I
see you woulde seeme to be that which you
are not, and as the prouerb sayth *Nodum in*
Cirpo quærere: Poetes you say vse coullors
to couer ther inconuiences, and wittie sentences to burnish theyr bawdery, and you diui-
nite to couer your knauerye. But tell mee
truth *Gosson* speakest thou as thou thinkest?
what coellers knowst thou in a Poete not to
be admitted? are his speaches vnperfect? sa-
uor they of inscience. I think if thou hast a-
ny shame thou canst not but like & approue
thē, are ther gods displesant vnto thee? doth
Saturne in his maiesty moue thee? doth *Iuno*
with

with her riches diſpleaſe thee:doth _Miner-_
_ua_ with her weapon diſcomfoꝛt thee? doth
Apollo with his harping harme thee? thou
mayſt ſay nothing les then harme thee becauſe they are not, and I thinke ſo to becauſe thou knoweſt them not. Foꝛ wot thou
that in the perſon of _Saturne_ our decaying
yeares are ſignified,in the picture of angry
Iuno,our affections are diſtiphered,in ẙ perſon of _Minerua_ is our vnderſtāding ſigniſi-
ed,both in reſpect of warre,as policie.when
they faine that _Pallas_ was begotten of the
bꝛaine of _Iupiter_ their meaning is none o-
ther, but that al wiſedome (as the learnꝛd
ſay) is from aboue, and commeth from the
father of Lights:in the poꝛtrature of _Apollo_
all knowledge is dedocated.ſo that, what ſo
they wꝛot,it was to this purpoſe,in the way
of pleaſure to dꝛaw men to wiſedome:foꝛ ſe-
ing the woꝛld in thoſe daies was vnperfect,
yt was neceſſary that they like good Phiſiti-
ons:ſhould ſo frame their potions, that they
might be appliable to the queſie ſtomaks of
their weriſh patients.but our ſtudientes by
your meanes haue made ſhipwꝛack of theyꝛ
laboꝛs,our ſchoolemaiſters haue ſo offended
that by your iudgement they ſhall _ſubire pæ_
nam capitis foꝛ teaching poetry,the vniuer-
ſitie is li.le beholding to you,al their pꝛacti-

A.z.   ces

res in teaching are friuolus . Witt hath
wrought that in you,that yeares and studie
neuer setled in the heads of our sagest doc-
tors.No meruel though you disprayse poetrye,when you know not what it meanes.
Erasmus will make that the path waye to
to knowledge which you disprayse, and no
meane fathers vouchsase in their seriouse
questions of deuinitie, to inserte poeticall
sensures . I think if we shal wel ouerloke y
Philosophers,we shal find their iudgemēts
not halfe persect , Poetes you saye fayle in
their fables,Philosophers in the verye se-
crets of Nature.Though Plato could wish
the expulsion of Poetes from his well pub-
liques,which he might doe with reason,yet
the wisest had not all that same opinion, it
had bene better for him to haue sercht more
narowly what the soule was,for his dissini-
tion was verye friuolus , when he would
make it naught els but Substantiam intelec-
tu predictam. if you say that Poetes did labour about nothing,tell me (I beseeh you)
what wonders wroughte those your dunce
Doctors in ther reasons de ente et non ente?
in they; definition of no force, and les witts
how sweate they power soules in makinge
more things then cold be? that I may vse
                                        your

your owne phrase, did not they spende one candle by seeking another. Democritus, Epicurus, with other scholler Metrodorus how labored they in finding out more worlds then one? your Plato in midst of his prescilines wrought that absurdite that neuer may be read in Poets, to make a yearthly creature to beare the person of the creator, and a corruptible substaunce, an incomprehensible God, for determining of the principall causes of all thinges, a made them naughte els but an Idea which if it be conferred wyth the truth, his sentence will sauour of Inscience. but I speake for Poets, I answeare your abuse, therefore I will disproue, or dispraise naught, but wish you with the wise Plato, to dispraise that thing you offend not in. Seneca sayth that the studdie of Poets, is to make children ready to the vnderstanding of wisedom, and that our aunciens did teache artes Eleutherias. i. liberales, because they instructed childre by the instrument of knowledg in time, became homines liberi. i. Philosophyc. it may be that in reding of poetry, it happened to you as it is with the Oyster, for shee in her swimming receiueth no apre, and you in your reading lesse instruction. it is reported that the sheepe of Enbois want ther galle, and

8

and one the contrarye ſide that the beaſtes of *Naxus* haue *diſtentum* fel. Men hope that ſcollers ſhould haue witt brought vpp in the Vniuerſite , but your ſweet ſelfe with the cattell of *Enboia*,ſince you left your College haue loſt your learning .you diſprayſe *Maximinns Tirius* pollicey,and that thinge that that he wrott to manifeſt learned Poets mening,you atribute to follye. O holy hedded man,why may not *Iuno* reſemble the ayre? why not *Alexander* valour ? why not *Vliſſes* pollice ? will you haue all for yon owne tothe?muſt men write that you maye know theyr meaning?as though your wytt were to wreſt all things? Alas ſimple *Irus*, begg at knowledge gate awhile, thou haſte not wonne the maſtery of learning . weane thy ſelfe to wiſedome, and vſe thy tallant in zeale not for enuie,abuſe not thy knowledge in diſprayſing that which is pereles:I ſhold bluſh from a player, to become an enuiouſe preacher,if thou hadſt zeale to preach, if for *Sions* ſake thou coldſt not holde thy tougue, thy true dealing were prayſe worthy,thy reuolcing woulde counſell me to reuerence thee.pittie weare it,that poetrye ſhould be diſplaced,full little could we want *Barbannans* workes, and *Boetius* comfortes may

not

not be baniſhed.wh	at made *Eraſmus* laboꝛ
in *Euripides* tragedies? did he indeuour by
painting them out of Greeke iuto Latine
to manifeſt ſinne vnto vs? oꝛ to confirme vs
in goodues? Laboꝛ (I pꝛay thee) in Pam-
phelets moꝛe pꝛayſe woꝛthy, thou haſte not
ſaued a Senꝛtoꝛ, therefoꝛe not woꝛthye ꝣ
Lawꝛell wꝛeth,thou haſt not(in diſpꝛouing
poetry) repꝛoued an abuſe,and therfoꝛe not
woꝛthy commendation. *Seneca* ſayth that
*Magna vitæ pars elabitur male agentibus,
maxima nibill agentibus, tota alind agentibus*, the moſt of our life (ſayd he) is ſpent e-
ther in doing euill, oꝛ nothing,or that wee
ſhould not,and I would wiſh you weare ex-
empted from this ſenſure, geue care but a
little moꝛe what may be ſaid foꝛ poetrie,foꝛ
I muſt be bꝛiefe, you haue made ſo greate
matter that I may not ſtay on one thing to
long,leſt I leaue an other vntouched. And
firſt whereas you ſay, ꝗ *Tullie* in his yeres
of moꝛe iudgement deſpiſed Poetes, harke
(I pꝛay you) what he woꝛketh foꝛ them in
his oꝛatiõ *pro Archia poeta* (but befoꝛe you
beare him leaſt you fayle in the incounter,
I would wyſh you to to ſullowe the aduiſe
of the daſterdlye *Ichneumon* of *Ægipt*, who
when ſhee beholdeth the *Aſpis* her enemye
to

to ᵭꝛawe nighe, calleth her fellowes toge=
ther, bismering her selfe with claye, againſt
the byting and ſtroke of the serpent, arme
your selfe, cal your witts together: want not
your wepons, leſt pour inperfect iudgement
be rewarded with Midas eares, you had
neede play the night-burd now, foꝛ your day
Owl hath misconned his parte, and foꝛ to
who now a dayes he cryes foole you: which
hath bꝛought such a soꝛt of wondering birds
about your eares, as I feare me will chat=
ter you out of your Iuey buſh. the woꝛlde
ſhames to see you, oꝛ els you are afrayde to
ſhew your selfe. you thought poetrye ſhould
want a patron (I think) when you fyꝛſte
publiſhed this inuectiue, but yet you fynd al
to many euē *preter expectationē*, yea though
it can speake foꝛ it selfe, yet her patron *Tullie* now ſhall tell her tale, *Hæc ſtudia* (ſayth
he) *adolescentiam alunt, Senectutem oblec-
tant, secundas res ornant, aduerſis perfugium
ac Solatium præbent, delectant domi, non im-
pediunt foris, pernoctant nobiscum, peregri-
antur, rusticantur*: then will you diſpꝛayse ẏ
which all men commend? you looke only vp
on ẏ refuse of ẏ abuse, nether respecting the
impoꝛtance of ẏ matter noꝛ the weighe of ẏ
wꝛꝑter. *Solon* can sayne himselfe madde, to
                                    further

further the *Athenians*. *Chaucer* in pleasant vain can rebuke sin vncontrold, & though he be lauish in the letter, his sence is serious. who in Rome lamented not *Roscius* death? & cast thou suck no plesure out of thy M. *Claudians* writings? hark, what *Cellarius* a learned father attributeth to it. *acuit memoriam* (saith he) it profiteth y memory. yea & *Tully* atributeth it for prais to *Archias* y vpon any theame he cold versify extempory. who liketh not of the promptnes of *Ouid*? who not vnworthely cold bost of himself thus *Quicquid conabar dicere versus erat.* who then dooth not wonder at poetry? who thinketh not y it proceedeth frō aboue? what made y *Chians* & *Colophonians* fal to such controuersy? Why seke y *Smirnians*, to recouer frō y *Salaminians* the prais of *Homer*? al wold haue him to be of ther city, I hope not for harme, but because of his knoledge. *Themistocles* desireth to be acquainted w those w could best discipher his praises. euen *Marius* himselfe, tho neuer so cruel, accōpted of *Plotinus* poems. what made *Aphricanus* esteme *Ennius*? why did *Alexander* giue prais to *Achilles* but for y praises which he found writte of hym by *Homer*? Why estemed *Pompie* so muche of *Theophanes Mitilres* or *Brutus* so greatlye the wrytinges *f Accius*? *Fuluius*

was

was so great a fauorer of poetry, that after
the Aetolian warres , he attributed to the
Muses those spoiles that belonged to *Mars*.
In all the Romaine conquest , hardest thou
euer of a slayne Poete? nay rather the Em-
perours honored them, beautified them with
benefites, & decked their sanctuaries which
sacrifice. *Pindarus* colledg is not fit for spoil
of *Alexander* ouercome, nether feareth poetry ye persecutors sword. what made Austin
so much affectate ye heauenly fury? not folly,
for if I must nerdes speake, *illud non ausim
affirmare*, his zeale was, in setting vp of the
house of God, not in affectate eloquence, he
wrot not , he accompted not, he honnored
not, so much that (famous poetry) whyche
we prayse , without cause, for if it be true
that *Horace* reporteth in his booke *de arte
poetica* , all the answeares of the Oracles
weare in verse. among the precise Iewes,
you shall find Poetes, and for more maiestie
Sibilla will prophesie in verse *Hiroaldus*
can witnes with me, that *Dauid* was a poet,
and that his vayne was in imitating (as S.
Ierom witnesseth) *Horace, Flaccus, & Pindarus*, somtimes his verse runneth in an *Iam-
bus* foote, anone he hath recourse to a *Saphi-
er* vaine, and *aliquando, semipede ingreditur*.
as h

aſk *Ioſephus*, and he wil tel you that Eſay,
Iob and Salomon, voutſafed poetical practi-
ſes, for (if *Origen* and he fault) not theyre
verſe was *Hexameter, and pentameter*. Enquire of *Caſſiodorus*, he will ſay that all the
beginning of Poetrye proceeded from the
Scripture. *Paulinus* tho the byſhop of *No-
lanum* yet voutſafe the name of a Poet, and
Ambroſe tho he be a patriarke in *mediolanū*
loueth verſifing *Beda* ſhameth not ÿ ſcience
that ſhameleſſe *Goſſon* miſliketh. reade ouer
Lactantius, his proofe is by poetry. ¶ Paul
voutſafeth to ouerlooke *Epimenides* let the
Apoſtle preach at Athens he diſdaineth not
of *Aratus* authorite. it is a prety ſentence
yet not ſo prety as pithy. *Poeta na ſcitur orator fit* as who ſhould ſay, Poetrye commeth
from aboue from a heauenly ſeate of a glo-
rious God vnto an excellent creature man,
an orator is but made by exerciſe. for if wee
examine well what befell *Ernius* amonge
the Romans, and *Heſiodus* among his con-
trimen the Gretians, howe they came by
theyr knowledge whence they receued their
heauenly furye, the firſt will tell vs that ſle-
ping vpon the Mount of *Parnaſſus* he dreamed that he receined the ſoule of *Homer* into him, after the which he became a Poete,
the

the next will assure you that it commeth not
by labor, nether that night watchings bryn-
geth it, but þ we must haue it thence whence
he fetched it w was (he saith) fro a wel of þ
Muses w Cabelimus calleth Poru, a draught
whereof drewe him to his perfection, so of a
shephard he becam an eloquet poet, wel the
you see þ it commeth not by exercise of play
making, nether insertio of gawds, but from
nature, and from aboue: and I hope þ Aristotle hath sufficiently taught you : that Na-
tura nihil fecit frustra. Perseus was made
a poete diuino furore percitus, and whereas
the poets were sayde to call for the Muses
helpe ther mening was no other as Iodocus
Badius reporteth, but to call for heauenly in
spiration from aboue to direct theyr ende-
reuors, nether were it good for you to sette
light by the name of a poet since þ oft pring
from whence he cometh is so heauenly, Sibil
la in hir answers to Æneas against hir will
as the poet telleth vs was possessed w thys
fury, ye wey consideratly but of the writing
of poets, & you shal se that whe ther matter
is most heauenly, their stile is most lostye, a
strange token of the wonderfull efficacy of
the same: I would make a long discourse i n
to you of Platoes 4. furies but I leue them
                                    it

it pitieth me to bring a rodd of your owne
making to beate you wythal, But methinks
whils you heare thys. I see you swallowe
downe your owne spittle for reuenge, wherᵉ
(God wot) my wryting saucreth not of en-
uye. in this case I coulde wyshe you fare
farre otherwyse from your foe yf you pleasᵉ
I wyll become your frewde and see what a
potion or receypt I can frame fytt for your
diet and herein I will proue my selfe a prac
tiser, before I purdge you, you shall take a
preparatiue to disburden your heauy heade
of those grose follis you haue conceued: but
the receipt is bitter, therfore I would wysh
you first to castell your mouth with the Suq-
ger of perseueráge: for ther is a cold rollop y
must downe your throate yet suche a one as
shall chasige your complection quit. I wyll
haue you therfore to tast first of y cold riuer
Phricus, in *Thracia* which as *Aristotle* reporteth changeth blacke into white, or of
Scamandar, which maketh gray yalow y
is of an enuious má a wel minded person, re
prehending of zeale y wherin he hath sinned
by folly, & so being prepard, thy purgation
wyll workes more easy, thy vnderstandinge
wyll be more persit, thou shalt blush at thy
abuse, and reclaime thy selfe by force of
argument

argument so will thou proue of clene reco-
uered patient, and I a perfecte practiser in
framing so good a potion. this broughte to
passe I with the wil seeke out some abuse
in poetry, which I wil seeke for to disproue
by reason first pronounced by no smal birde
euen *Aristotle* himself *Poetæ* (sayth he) *mul-
ta mentiuntur* and to further his opinion seuer *Cato* putteth in his centure.

Admiranda canunt sed non credenda poetæ.
these were sore blemishes if obiected right-
ly and heare you may say the streme rinnes
a wronge, but if it be so by you leue I wyll
bring him shortly in his right chanel. My
answere shall not be my owne, but a learned
father shall tell my tale, if you wil know his
name men call him *Lactantius:* who in hys
booke de *diuinis institutionibus* reesoneth
thus. I suppose (sayth he) Poets are full of
credit, and yet it is requesite for those that
wil vnderstand them to be admonished, that
among them, not onely the name but the
matter beareth a show of that it is not: for if
sayth he we examine the Scriptures litter-
allye nothing will seeme more falls, and if
we way Poetes wordes and not ther meaning, our learning in them wilbe very mene
you see nowe that your *Catoes* iudgement
                                              as

of no force and that all your obiections you
make agaynst poetrye be of no valor yet lest
you should be altogether discoraged I wyll
helpe you forwarde a little more, it pities
me to consider the weaknes of your cause I
wyll therfore make your strongest reason,
more stroug and after I haue builded it vp
destroy it agayn. Poets you confesse are el-
oquent but you reproue them in their wantonnesse, they write of no wisedom, you may
say their tales are friuolus, they prophane
holy thinges, they seeke nothing to the perfection of our soules. theyr practise is in o-
ther things, of lesse force: to this obiection I
answer no otherwise then Horace doeth in
his booke *de arte poetica* where he wryteth
thus.

Siluestres homines sacer interpresque deorum
Sedibus, et victu soedo deterruit orpheus.
Dictus ob hoc lenire Tigres rabidosque leones.
Dictus et Amphion Thebanæ condit vrbis
Saxa mouere sono, testudis et prece blanda
Ducere quo vellet fuit hoc sapientia quondam.
Publica priuatis secernere sacra prophanis.
Concubitu prohibere vago, dare Iura maritis,
Opida moliri leges, niscidere ligno.

The holy spokesman of the Gods
With heauely Orpheus hight:
Did driue the sauage men from wods,

And

And made them liue aright.
And therfore is sayd the Tygers fierce,
And Lyons full of myght
To ouercomet Amphion, he
Was sayd of Theabs the founder,
Who by his force of Lute dyd cause,
The stones to part a sonder.
And by his speach them did derect.
Where he would haue them stayet
This wisedome this was it of olde
All strife for to allay.
To giue to euery man his owne,
To make the Gods be knowne
To dryue each lecher from the bed,
That neuer was his owne.
To teach the law of mariage,
The way to build a towne,
For to engraue these lawes in woods
This was these mens renowne.
I cannot leaue Tirtheus pollicy vntouched,
who by force of his pen could incite men to
the defence of theyr countrye. if you require
of ý Oracle of Apollo what successe you shal
haue? respondet bellicoso numine lo now you
see your obiections my answers, you behold
or may perceiue manifestlye, that Poetes
were the first raysors of cities, prescribers of
good lawes, maynteyners of religion, distur
bors

boys of the wicked, aduancers of the wel dis∙
posed, inuctors of laws, & lastly the very fot
paths to knowledg, & vnderstāding ye if we
sholo beleue Herome he wil make *Platos* ex
iles honest mē, & his pestiferous poets good
preachers: for he accounteth *Orpheus Mus-
eus*, & *Linus*, *Christians*, therefore *Virgil* (in
his 6. boke of *Æneiados*) wher he lernedly de
scribeth þ iourny of *Æneas* to *Elisum*) asser∙
teneth vs, þ among them þ were ther for the
zeale they beare toward there country, ther
wer found *Quinque pij vates et Phæbo digna
loquti* but I must answer al obiectiōs, I must
fil euery nooke, I must arme my self now, for
here is the greatest bob I can gather out of
your boke forsoth *Ouids abuses*, in descry∙
bing whereof you labour very vehementlye
termīg him lectcher, & in his person dispraise
all poems, but shall on mans follye destroye
à vniuersal cōmodity? what gife what perfit
knowledg hath ther bin, emong þ professors
of wt ther hath not bin a bad, on the Angels
haue sinned in heauē, *Ada* & *Eur* in earthly pa
radise, omōg þ holy apostles vngratious Iu
das, I resōn not þ al poets are holy but I af
firme þ poetry is a beauūly gift, a perfit gift
ever wt I know noc greater plesure, & surely
tf I may speak my mind I thīk we shal finc

B.2.   but

but few poets if it were exactly wayd what
they oughte to be pour *Muscouian* straun-
gers, pour *Scithian* monsters wonderful by
one *Eurus* brought vpon one stage in ships
made of Sheepeskins, wyll not proue you a
poet nether pour life alow you to bee of that
learning if you had wisely wayed ÿ abuse of
poetry if you had reprehended ÿ foolish fan-
tasies of our poets *nomine non re* which they
bring fozth on stage, my self wold haue liked
of you & allowed pour laboz. but I perceiue
nowe ÿ all red colloured stones are not Ru-
bies, nether is euery one *Alexandar* ÿ hath
a stare in his cheke, al lame men are not *V-*
ulcans, noz hooke nosed men. *Ciceroes* nether
each professer a poet. I abhoze those poets
that sauoz of ribaldzy, I will with the zealous admit the expulsion of suche enozmi-
ties poetry is dispzaised not foz the folly that
is in it, but foz the abuse whiche manye ill
Wzyters couler vp it. Beleeue mee the
magestrats moy take aduise, (as I knowe
wisely can) to roote out those odde rymes
which runnes in euery rascales mouth. Sa-
uozing of rybaldzy, those foolish balleds,
that are admired. Make poets good and
godly practises to be refused. I like not of a
wicked *Nero* that wyll expell *Lucan*, yet ad-
                                        mit

mit J of a zealous gouernour that wil seke
to take away the abuse of poetry. J like not
of an angrye *Augustus* which wyll banishe
Ouid for enuy, Jloue a wise Senator, which
in wisedome wyll correct him and with aduise burne his follyes: vnhappy were we yf
like poore *Scaurus* we shoulde find *Tiberius*
that wyll put vs to death for a tragedy making but most blessed were we, if we n.ight
find a iudge that seuerely would amende the
abuses of Tragedies, but J leaue the refor-
mation thereof to more wyser than my selfe,
And retourne to Gosson whom J wyshe to
be fully perswaded in this cause, and therefore J will tell hym a prety story, which *Iu-
stin* wryteth in the prayse of poetrye. The
Lacedemonians when they had loste many
men in diuers incountryes with theyr enemyes soughte to the Oracles of Apollo re-
quiring how they myght recouer theyr losses, it was answered that they mighte ouercome if so be that they could get an *Atheni-
an* gouernor, whereupon they sent Orators
vnto the *Athenians* humbly requesting them
that they woulde appoynt them out one of
theyr best captaynes: the *Athenians* owinge
them old malice, sent them in steede of a sol-
dada vecbio a scholar of the Muses. in steede
of

of a worthy warrior a poore poet, for a cou-
ragious *Themistocles* a silly *Tirthetus* , a
man of great eloquence and singuler wytte,
yet was he but a lame lymde captaine more
fit for the coche then the field, the *Lacedemonians* trusting the Oracle, recued the cham-
pion, and fearing the gouernment of a stran-
ger, made him ther Citizen. which once don
and he obteining the Dukdome, he assended
the theater, and ther very learnedly) wysh-
ing them to forget theyr folly, and to thinke
on victory they being acuate by his eloquece
waging battail won the fielde. Lo now you
see that the framing of common welthes, &
defence therof, proceedeth from poets, how
dare you therfore open your mouth against
them? how can you dispraise the preseruer
of a countrye? you compare *Homer* to *Me-
thecui*, cookes to Poetes, you shame your
selfe in your vnreuerent similituds, you may
see your follyes *verbum sapienti sat*. where
as *Homar* was an ancient poet, you disalow
him, and accompte of those of lesser iudgement. *Strabo* calleth poetry, *primam sapi-
entiam*. *Cicero* in his firste of hys Tuscu-
lans attributeth p inuencion of philosophy,
to poets. God keepe vs from a Plato that
should expel such men. pittie were it that the
memo-

memozy of thefe valiant victours ſhould be
hidden, whtch haue dyed in the behalfe of
ther countryes:miſerable were our ſtate yf
we wanted thoſe wozthy volumes of poetry
could the learned beare the loſſe of Homers?
oz our younglings the wzytings of Man-
tuan?oz you your volumes of hiſtozyes? beleue me yf you had wanted your Myſteries
of nature,& your ſtately ſtozyes, your booke
would haue ſcarce bene tedde wyth matter:
if therefoze you will deale in things of wiſ-
dome, cozrect the abuſe,honoz the ſcience,re
newe your ſchoole, crye out ouer Hieru-
ſalem wyth the pzophet,the woe that he pzo
nounced, with the teacher to refozme hys
lyfe,that his weake ſcholler may pzoue the
wyſer,cry out againſt vnſaciable delyze in
rich men,tel the houſe of Jacob theyz iniqui
ties,lament with the Apoſtle the want of
labozers in the Lozds vineyards,cry out on
thoſe dume doggs that will not barke, wylt
the mightye that they ouermayſter not the
pooze,and put downe the beggers pzowde
heart by thy perſwaſions. Thunder oute
wyth the Pzophete Micha the meſage
of the LORD, and wyth hym delyze
the Judges to heare thee , the Pzynces
of Jacob to hearken to thee, and thoſe of
B.4.   the

the house of Israell to vnderstande then tell
them that they abhozre iudgement, and pze-
uent equitie, that they iudge foz rewardes,
and that theyz pzielts teach foz hyze, and the
pzophets thereof pzophesie foz money , and
yet that they saye the Lozde is wyth them,
and that no euil can befall them, bzeath out
the sweete pzomises to the good, the curlses
to the bavde, tell them that a peeace multe
needes haue a warre , and that God can
rayse vp another Zenacharib, shew thē that
Salamons kingdome was but foz a season and that aduerlitie cometh ere we elpye
it, these be the songes of Sion, these be those
rebukes which you oughte to add to abuses
recouer the body, foz it is soze, the appedices
thereof will easely be reformed, if that wear
at a staye, but other matter call me and I
mult not staye vpon this onely, there is an
easier task in hand foz me, and that which if
I may speak my conscience, fitteth my vain
bett, your second abuse Gosson, your second
abuse pour dispzayses of Mulik, which you
vnaduisedly terme pyping : that is it wyll
mott byte you, what so is a ouerstay of life,
is displesant to your person, mulik may not
ttand in your pzesence, whereas all the lear
ned Philosophers haue alwayes had it in
reuerence,

reuerence. *Homar* commendeth it highly, referring to the prayses of the Gods whiche
Gosson accompteth folishnesse, looke vppon
the harmonie of the Heauens? hange they
not by Musike? doe not the *Spheares* moue?
the *primus* motor gouerne. be not they *in-
feriora corpora* affected *quadam sumpathia*
and agreement? howe can we measure the
debilitie of the patient but by the disordered
motion of the pulse? is not man worse accompted of when he is most out of tune? is
there any thinge that more affecteth the
sence? doth there any pleasure more acuat
our vnderstanding. can the wonders y hath
wroughte and which you your selfe confesse
no more moue you? it sitteth well nowe that
the learned haue sayd, *musica requirit gene-
rosum animū* which since it is far from you,
no maruel though you fauor not that profession. it is reported of the *Camelion* that shee
can chaunge her selfe vnto all coollors saue
whyte, and you can accompte of all thinges
saue such as haue honesty . *Plutarch* your
good Maysster may bare me witnes , that
the ende whereto Musick was, will proue
it prayes worthy, O Lorde howe maketh it
a man to remember heauenly things. to wō-
der at the works of the creator, *Eloquence*
can

can ſtay the ſouldiars ſwoꝛde from ſlayinge
an Oꝛatoꝛ,and ſhall not muſike be magni-
fied which not onely ſaueth the bodye but is
a comfoꝛt to the ſoule? Dauid reiopſeth ſingeth and pꝛayſeth the Loꝛde by the Harpe,
the Simbale is not remoued from his ſanc
tuary,the Aungels ſyng *gloria in excelſis*.
Surely the imagination in this pꝛeſent in-
ſtant,calleth me to a deepe conſideration of
my God. looke foꝛ wonders where muſike
woꝛketh,and wher harmonie is ther folow-
eth increcible delectation. the bowels of the
earth yeld.where the inſtrument ſoundeth
and *Pluto* cannot keepe *Proſerpina* if *Orpheus* recoꝛde. The Seas ſhall not ſwallowe
Arion whilſt he ſingeth,nether ſhall hee pe-
riſh while he harpeth,a doleſul tuner pf a di-
ing muſition can moue a Monſter of ꝑ ſea.
to mourne. a Dolphin reſpectet a heauen-
lye recoꝛde. call your ſelfe home therefoꝛe
and reclayme thys follye, it is to foule to
bee admitted,you may not mayntaine it.I
hadd well hoped you woulde in all theſe
thynges haue wiſelye admytted the thyng,
and diſalowe naughte but the abuſe , but
I ſee your mynde in your wꝛytinge was
to penn ſomewhat you knowe not what,
and

fra.2

and to con⸗firme it I wot not howe, so that
your selfe hath hatched vꝫ an Egge yet so
that it hath blest vs wyth a monsterus chic-
kin, both wythoute hedde, and also taple,
lyke the Father, full of imperfec:ion and
lesse zeale, well marke yet a lyttle moꝛe,
beare with me though I be bytter, my loue
is neuer the lesse foꝛ that I haue learned of
Tullye, that *Nulla remedia tam faciunt
dolorem quam quæ sunt salutaria*, the sharper medycine the better it cures, the moꝛe
you see your follye, the sooner may you a-
mende it. Are not the straines in Musike
to tickle and delyght the eare? are not our
warlike instruments to moue men to valoꝛ?
You confesse they mooue vs, but yet they
delight not our eares, I pꝛay you whence
grew that poynt of Phylosophy? it is moꝛe
then euer my Maysſter taught mee, that a
thynge of sounde shoulde not delyghte the
eare. belyke yee suppose that men are monsters, withoute eares, oꝛ else I thynke you
wyll saye they beare with theyre heeles,
it may bee so, foꝛ indeede when wee are
are delighted with Musike, it maketh our
heart to skypp foꝛ ioye, and it mayt bee
perhaps by assending from the heele to the
hygher partes. it may moue vs, good
                                        policie

policy in sooth, this was of your owne cop=
ning your mother neuer taught it you, but
I wyll not deale by reason of philosophye
wyth you for that confound your sences, but
I can asure you this one thinge, that this
principle will make the wiser to mislike
your inuention, it had bene a fitter iest for
your howlet in your playe, then an ornamēt
in your booke. but since you wrote of abuses
we may licence you to lye a little, so ŷ abuse
will be more manifest. lord with how good=
ly a cote haue you clothed your conceiptes,
you abound in storyes but impertinent, they
bewray your reeding but not your wisedom
would God they had bin well aplyed. But
now I must play the musitian right nolesse
buggs now come in place but pauions and
mesures, dumps & fancies & here growes a
great question, what musick *Homer* vsed in
curing ŷ diseased gretians, it was no dump
you say, & so think I, for ŷ is not apliable to
sick men, for it fauoreth Malancholie. I am
sure, it was no mesure, for in those days they
were not such good dāsers for sooth thē what
was it? if you require me. if you name me the
instrumēt, I wyl tel you what was ŷ musik.
mean while a gods name let vs both dout, ŷ
it is no part of our saluation to know what it
was

was no2 how it went? when I speak wyth
Homer next you shall knowe his answere.
But you can not be content to erre but you
must maintain it to. *Pithagoras* you say a-
lowes not that musik is decerned by eares,
but hee wisheth vs to assend vnto the skye &
marke that harmony. surely thys is but one
docto2s opinion (yet I dislike not of it) bnt
to speake my conscience my thinkes musike
best pleaseth me when I heare it, fo2 otherwise the catter walling of Cats, were it not
fo2 harmonie: should mo2e delight mine eies
then the tunable voyces of men. but these
things are not the chiefest poynts you shote
at, thers somewhat els sticketh in your sto-
mak God graunt it hurt you not, from the
daunce you runn to the pype, from 7. to 3.
which if I shoulde add I beleeue I coulde
w2est out halfe a sco2e incouueniences mo2e
out of your booke. our pleasant conso2tes do
discomfo2t you much, and because you lyke
not thereof, they arr discomendable, I haue
heard it is good to take sure fotinge when
we trauel bnknowen countryes, fo2 when
we wade aboue our shoe latchet *Appelles*
wyll rep2ehende vs fo2 coblers, if you had
bene a father in musick and coulde haue de-
serued of tunes I would perhaps haue like
                                        your

your opinion sumwhat where now I abhor
it,if you wear a profeſſor of that practiſe I
would quickly perſwade you,that the ad-
ding of ſtrings to our inſtrument make the
ſound more hermonious,and that the mix-
ture of Muſike maketh a better concent.but
to preach to vnſkillfull is to perſwad ẏ braue
beaſtes, I wyl not ſtand long in thys point
although the dignitye thereof require a volume,but howe learned men haue eſteemed
this heauenly gift,if you pleaſe to read you
ſhall ſee.Socrates in hys old age will not diſ-
dayn to learn ẏ ſcience of Muſik amõg chil-
ren,he can abide their correctiõs to;ſo much
accoũted he that,w̃ you contemn.ſo profi a-
ble thoughte he ẏ, w̃ you miſlik.Solon wil e-
ſteme ſo much of ẏ knowledg of ſinging,ẏ he
wil ſoner forget to dye then to ſing. Pithagoras liks it ſo wel ẏ he wil place it in Greace.
aud Ariſtoxenus will ſaye ẏ the ſoule is muſik ẏ Plato(in his booke de legibus) will affirme that it can not be handled wichout all
ſciences,the Lacedemonians ẏ Creteaſis wer
ſturred to warre by Anapeſtus foote, and
Timotheus with the ſaine incenſed kinge
Alexander to bател,ye yf Boetyus ſitten not
on Tautomicuaus(:by this Phrigian ſound ẏ
baſſen vto hñin ahouſe uher a ſtruрet was
bidden.ſo litle abideth this heauẽly harmony

out

our humane filthines, þ it worketh wonders
as you may perceue most manifestly by the
history of *Agamemnon* who going to þ Troi-
an war, left at home a musitian þ playde the
Dorian tune, who wᵗ the foote *Spondeus* pre-
serued his wife *Clitemnestra* in chastity & honesty, wherfore she cold not bee deflowred
by *Ægistus*, before he had wickedly slain the
musitian. so þ as the magnetes draweth Iron-
ne, & the Theamides (wᶜ groweth in *Ægipt*)
driueth it away: so musik calleth to it selfe al
honest plesures, & dispelleth frō it all vaine
misdemanors. þ matter is so plētiful that I
cannot find wher to end, as for beginnings
they be infinite, but these shall suffice. I like
not to long circūstances wher les doe serue:
only I wish you to accoumpt wel of this hea-
uēly concent, wᶜ is ful of perfettiō, proceding
frō aboue, drawing his original frō the motion of þ stars, frō the agrement of the planets, frō the whisteling winds & frō al those
celestial circles, where is ether perfit agree-
mēt or any *Sumphonia*, but as I like musik
so admit I not of thos that depraue the same
your pipers are, as odius to mee as your
selfe, nether alowe I your harpinge mery
beggers: although I knewe you my selfe a
professed play maker, & a paltry actor. since
which þ windmil of your wit hath bin tornd
so

so long wyth the wynde of folly, that I feare
me we shall see the dogg returne to his vo-
mit, and the clensed sow to her myre, and the
reformed scholemayster to hys old teaching
of folly. beware it be not so, let not your
booke be a blemish to your own profession.
Correct not musik therfore whē it is prayes
worthy, least your worthlesse misliking bewray your madnes. way the abuse and that
is matter sufficient to serue a magistrates
animaduersion . heere may you abuse
well, and if you haue any stale rethorik florish vpon thys text, the abuse is, when that
is a pplyed to wantonnesse , which was
created to shewe Gods worthinesse. When
y shamefull resorts of shameles curtezanes
in sinful sonnets , shall prophane vertue
these are no light sinnes, these make many
goodmen lament, this cauleth parents hate
there right borne children, if this were reformed by your policie I should esteme of you
as you wysh. I feare me it fareth far other
wyse, *latet anguis in herba*, vnder your fare
show of conscience take heede you cloakt
not your abuse , it were pittie the learned
should be ouerseene in your simplenesse , I
feare me you will be politick wyth *Macha-
uel* not zealous as a prophet. Well I will
not

not stay long vpon the abuse, for that I see it is to manifest, the remembraunce thereof is discommendable among the godly, and I my self am very loth to bring it in memory. to the wise aduised reader these mai suffice, to flee the *Crocodel* before hee commeth, lest we be bitten, and to auoyde the abuse of musik, since we se it, lest our misery be more When we fall into folly. *I Ekus piscator fa-pit.* you heare open confession, these abuses are disclaimed by our Gosson, he is sory that hee hath so leudlye liued, & spent the oyle of his perfection in vnsaucry Lampes. he hath *Argus* eyes to watch him now, I wold wish him beware of his Islington, and such lyke resorts, if now he retourne from his repen-ted lyfe to his old folly, Lord how foule wil be his fall. men know more then they speak if they be wise, I feare me some will blushe that readeth this, if he be bitten. wold God Gosson, at that instant might haue a watch-man. but I see it were needelesse, perhaps he hath *Os durum,* and then what aua pleth their prelence. Well, I leaue this poynt til I know further of your mynde, mean while I must talke a little wyth you about ẙ thyrd abuse, for the cater cosens of pypers, theyr names (as you terme them) be players, & I

C.   think

thinke as you doe, fo2 your experience is suf
ficient to enfo2me me. but here I must loke
about me, *quacunque te tigeris vicus est,* here
is a task that requireth a long treatis, and
what my opinion is of players ye now shall
plainly perceue. I must now serch my wits,
I see this shall passe th2 oughe many seuere
senso2s handling, I must aduise me what I
w2ite, and w2ite that I would wysh. I way
wel the seriousnes of the cause, and regarde
berymuch the Iudges of my endeuo2, whom
if I could I would perswade, that I woulde
not nourish abuse, nether maymtaine that
which should be an vniuersall discomoditye.
I hope they wil not iudge befo2e they read,
nether condemne without occasion The wisest wil alwais carry to eares, in p they are
to diserne two indifferent causes. I meane
not to hold you in suspec, (seuere Iudges) if
you gredely expect my verdit b2efely this it
is.

Demostines thoughte not that *Thillip*
shoulde ouercome when he rep2oued hym,
nether feared *Cicero Anthonies* fo2ce, when
in the Senate hee rebuked hym. To the ig-
no2ant ech thinge that is vnknowne semes
Vnp2ofitable, but a wise man can fo2esee and
p2ayse by p2oofe. *Pythagoras* could spy oute
in

in womens eyes two kind of teares, the one
of grefe the other of disceit: & those of iudge
ment can from the same flower suck honey
with the bee, from whence the Spyder (I
mean the ignorant) take their poison. men y
haue knowledge what comedies & tragedis
be, wil comend thē, but it is sufferable in the
folish to reproue that they know not, becaus
ther mouthes wil hardly be stopped. Firste
therfore if it be not tedious to Gosson to har
ken to the lerned, the reder shal perceiue the
antiquity of playmaking, the inuentors of
comedies, and therewithall the vse & como-
ditye of thē. So that in y end I hope my labor shall be liked, and the learned wil soner
conceiue his folly. For tragedies & comedies
Donate the gramarian sayth, they wer inuen
ted by lerned fathers of the old time to no o-
ther purpose, but to peelde prayse vnto God
for a happy haruest, or plentifull yeere. and
that thys is trewe the name of Tragedye
doeth importe, for if you consiuer whence
it came, you shall perceiue (as *Iodocus
Badius* reporteth) that it drewe his original
of *Tragos, Hircus,* & *Ode, Cantus,* (so called)
for that the actors thereof had in rewarde
for theyr labour, a Gotes skynne fylled
wyth wyne. You see then that the fyrste

C.2.   matter

matter of Tragedies was to giue thankes
and prayses to GOD, and a gratefull
prayer of the countrymen for a happye
haruest. and this I hope was not discommendable. I knowe you will iudge is farthest from abuse. but to wade farther, thys
fourme of inuention being found out, as the
dayes wherein it was vsed did decay, and
the world grew to more perfection, so y witt
of the younger sorte became more riper, for
they leauing this fourme, inuented an other,
in the which they altered the nature but not
y name: or for sonnets in prayse of y gods,
they did set forth the sower fortune of many
exiles, the miserable fal of haples princes,
The reuinous decay of many coutryes, yet
not content with this, they presented the
liues of _Satyers_. So that they might wiselye
vnder the abuse of that name, discouer the fol
lies of many theyr folish fellow citesens. and
those monsters were then, as our parasites
are now adayes: suche, as with pleasure reprehended abuse. as for commedies because
they bear a more plesanter vain, I wil leaue
the other to speake of them. _Tully_ defines
them thus. _Comedia_ (saith he) is _Imitatio_
vitæ, speculum consuetudinis, & imago veri-
tatis. and it is sayde to be termed of _Comai_,
(emongst

(embngste the Greckes) whiche signifieth
Pagos,& *Ode*,*Cantus* : foz that they were ex-
ercised in the fielde. they had they beginning
wyth tragedies, but their matter was moze
plessaunt, foz they were suche as did repze-
hend, yet *quodam lepore*. These first very rud-
ly were inuented by *Susarion Bullus*,& *Mag-
nes*, to auncient poets, yet so, that they were
meruelous pzofitable to the reclampnge of
abuse : whereupon *Eupolis* with *Cartinus*,&
Aristophanes, began to wzite, and with ther
eloquenter baine and perfection of stil, dyd
moze seuerely speak agaynst the abuses that
they: which *Horace* himselfe witnesseth. Foz
sayth he ther was no abuse but these men re-
pzehended it. a these was loth to be seene one
there spectacle. a coward was neuer pzesent
at theyz assemblies. a backbiter abhozd that
companp, and I my selfe could not haue bla
med pour (Gosson) foz exempting pour selfe
from this theater , of troth I should haue
lykt pour pollitp. These therefoze, these wer
they that kept men in awe, these restrayned
the vnbzidled cominaltie, wherupon *Horace*
wisely sayeth.

Oderunt peccare boni, virtutis amore.
Oderunt peccare mali, formidine pene.

The

The good did hate al sinne for vertues loue
The bad for feare of shame did sin remoue.

Yea would God our realme could light vppon a *Lucillius*, then should the wicked bee
poynted out from the good, a harlot woulde
secke no harbor at stage plais, lest she shold
here her owne name growe in question: and
the discourse of her honesty cause her to bee
hated of the godly. as for you I am sure of
this one thing, he would paint you in your
players ornaments, for they best beeam you.
But as these sharpe corrections were disa-
nulde in Rome when they grewe to more
licenciousnes: So I feare me if we shold prac
tise it in our dayes, the same intertainmente
would followe. But in ill reformed Rome
what comedies now? a poets wit can correct, yet not offend. *Philemon* will mitigate
the corrections of sinne, by reprouing them
couertly in shadowes. *Menander* dare not
offend ÿ Senate openly, yet wants he not a
parasite to touch them priuely. *Terence* wyl
not report the abuse of harlots vnder there
proper stile, but he can finely girde thē vnder
the person of *Thais*. hee dare not openly tell
the Rich of theyr couetousnesse and seuerity
towards their children, but he can controle
them

them vnder the perſon of *Durus Demear*, he
muſt not ſhew the abuſe of noble yong gen‑
tilmen vnder theyr owne title, but he wyll
warne them in the perſon of *Pamphilus*.wil
you learne to know a paraſite? Looke vpon
his *Davus*.wyl you ſeke the abuſe of courtly
flatterers?behold *Gnato*.and if we had ſome
Satericall Poetes nowe a dayes to penn
our commedies, that might be admitted of
zeale,to diſcypher the abuſes of the worlde
in the perſon of notorious offenders.I know
we ſhould wiſely ryd our aſſemblyes of ma‑
ny of your brotherhod.but becauſe you may
haue a full ſcope to reprehende, I will ryp
vp a rablement of playmakers,wheſe wrigh‑
tinges I would wiſhe you ouerlooke. and
ſeeke out theyr abuſes. can you miſlike of
Cecilius? or diſpiſe *Plinius*.? or amend *Ne‑
uius*?or find fault with *Licinius*?where in of‑
fended *Attilius*? I am ſure you can not but
wonder at *Terrence*?wil it pleaſe you to like
of *Turpelius*? or alow of *Trabea*?you muſte
needs make much of *Ennius* for ouerloke al
thes,& you ſhal find ther volums ful of wit if
you examin thē:ſo þ if you had no other maſ‑
ters,you might deſerue to be a doctor,wher
now you are but a foliſhe ſcholemaiſter.but
I wyll deale wyth you verye freendlye,

C.4.   I

I wil refolue eueri doubt that you find, thofe
inſtrumentes which you miſlike in playes
grow of auncient cuſtome, foʒ when Roſſius
was an Actoʒ, be ſure that as with his tears
he moued affections, ſo the Muſitian in the
Theater befoʒe the entrance, did moʒnefully
recoʒd it in melody (as Seruius repoʒteth.)
Theactoʒs in Rome had alſo gay clothinge
euery mãs aparel was apliable to his part
ʒ perſon. The old men in white, ʒ rich men
in purple, the paraſite diſguiſedly, the yong
men in goʒgeous coulours, ther wanted no
deuiſe noʒ good iudgemẽt of ʒcomedy, whẽ
J ſuppoſe our players, both dʒew ther plaies ʒ fourme of garments, as foʒ the appointed dayes wherin comedies wer ſhowen, J
reede that the Romaynes appoynted them
on the feſtiual dayes, in ſuch repuſation
were they had at that tune . Alſo Iodocus
Badius will aſſertain you that the actoʒs foʒ
ſhewing pleaſure receued ſome pʒofite. but
let me apply thoſe dayes to ours, their actoʒs to out players, their autoʒs to ours.
ſurely we want not a Roſſius, nether at ther
great ſcarſity of Terrences pʒofeſſiõ, but yet
tur then dare not nowe a dayes pʒeſume ſo
much, as the old Poets might. and therfoʒe
they apply ther wʒiting to the peoples vain
                                    where

wheras,if in the beginning they had ruled,
we should now adaies haue found smal spectacles of folly.but (of truth) I must confesse
with *Aristotle*,that men are greatly delighted with imitation,and that it were good to
bring those things on stage,that were al together tending to vertue:all this I admit,&
hartely wysh,but you say vnlesse the thinge
be taken away the vice will continue,nay I
say if the style were changed the practise
would profit,and sure I thinke our theaters
fit,that *Ennias* seeing our woaton *Glicerium*
may rebuke her,if our poetes will nowe become seuere,and for prophaue things write
of vertue:you I hope shoulde see a reformed
state in those thinges, which I feare me yf
they were not, the idle hedded commones
would worke more mischiefe.I with as zea-
lously as the best that all abuse of playinge
weare abolished,but for the thing,the anti-
quitie causeth me to allow it,so it be vsed as
it should be. I cannot allow the prophaning
of the Sabaoth, I praise your reprehension
in that, you did well in discommending the
abuse,and surely I wysh that that folly were
disclaymed,it is not to be admitted,it maks
those sinnes whiche perhaps if it were not,
would haue bixne present at a good sermon.
it

it is in the Magistrate to take away that o2
der,and appoynt it otherwyse. but sure it
were pittie to abolish ẙ which hath so great
vertue in it.because it is abused. The Ger-
manes when the vse of p2eaching was fo2-
bidden them, what helpe had they I p2ay
you?fo2soth the learned were fayne couertly
in comodies to declare abuses, and by playing to incite the people to vertues,whē they
might heare no p2eaching.Those were la-
mentable dayes you will say, and so thinke
I,but was not this I p2ay you a good help
in refo2ming the decaying Gospel? you see
then how comedies (my seuere iudges) are
requesit both fo2 ther antiquity,and fo2 ther
commoditye. fo2 the dignity of the w2igh-
ters,and the pleasure of the hearers. But
after your discrediting of playmaking, you
salue vppon the so2e somewhat,and among
many wise wo2kes there be some that fitte
your vaine:the p2actise of pa2asites is one,
which I meruel it likes you so well since it
bites you so so2e.but sure in that I like your
iudgement, and fo2 the rest to, I app2oue
your wit,but fo2 the pigg of your own sow,
(as you terme it) assuredly I must discom-
mend your verdit, tell me Gosson was all
your owne you w2ote there: did you borow
                                        nothing

nothing of your neyghbours? out of what
booke patched you out *Ciceros oration* ?
whence fet you *Catulins* inuectiue. Thys is
one thing, *alienam olet lucernà non tuam.* fo
that your helper may wifely reply vpon you
with *Virgil*.

Hos ego verſiculos feci tulit alter honores.

I made thefe verfes other bear the name,
beleue me I fhould preferr Wilfons fhorte
and fweete if I were iudge, a peece furely
worthy prayfe, the practife of a good fchol-
ler, would the wifer would ouerlooke that,
they may perhaps cull fome wifedome, out
of a players toye. Well, as it is wifedome
to commend where the caufe requireth, fo it
is a poynt of folly to praife without deferte,
you diflike players very much, theyr dea-
lings be not for your commodity, whom if
I myghte aduife they fhould learne thys of
Iuuenal.

Viuendum eſt, rectè
cum propter plurimæ, tum bis
Præcipue eiuſis vt linguas mancipiorum
Contæas. Na lingua mali pars peſſima ſeruiẏ

We ought to leade our lines aright,

For

For many causes moue,
Especially for this same cause,
Wisedome doth vs behone.
That we may set at nough those blames,
Which seruants to vs lay,
For why the tongue of euel slaue,
Is worst as wisemen euer say.

Methinks I heare some of them versifing
these verses vpon you, if it be so that I hear
them, I wil concele it, as for the statute of
apparrell and the abuses therof, I see it manifestly broken.and if I should seeke for example, you cannot but offend my eyes. For
if you examine the statuts exactly, a simple
cote should be fitted to your backe. we sholo
bereue you of your brauerye, and examine
your ancestry, & by profession in respect of ẙ
statute, we should find you catercosens with
a, (but hush) you know my meaning, I must
for pitie fauor your credit in that you weare
once a scholler. you runne farther to Carders, dicers, fencers, bowlers, daunsers, &
tomblers. whose abuses I wold rebuke with
you, had not your self moued other matters.
but to eche I say thus, for dicing I wyshe
those that know it not to leaue to learn it, &
let the fall of others make them wiser. Yf

they had an *Alexander* to gouern they shold,
be punished, and I could wish them not to a-
buse the lenitie of their prince. *Cicero* for a
great blemish reputeth that which our gen-
tilmen vse for brauery, but *sufficit ista leui-
ter attigisse*, a word against fencers, & so an
end, whom I wish to beware with *Demonax*
lest admitting theyr fencing delightes, they
destroy (with the *Athenians*) the alters of
peace, by rapling quarrellous causes, they
worke vprores: but you and I reproue thē
in abuse, yet I (for my part) cannot but allow the practise so it be well vsed, as for the
filling of onr gracious princes cofers with
peace, as it pertaineth not to me, because I
am none of her receiuors, so men think vnlesse it hath bine lately you haue not bene of
her maiesties counsel. But now here as you
begin folishly, so surely you end vnlernedly.
preser you warre before peace? the sword before the Goune ? the rule of a Tyrant, before y happy days of our gracious Queen?
you know the philosophers are against you,
yet dare you stand in handygrips wyth *Cicero*: you know that force is but an instrumēt
when counsell fayleth, and if wisedome win
not, farwel warre . Aske *Alphonsus* what
counsellors he lyketh of ? hee will say his
bookes?

bookes. and hath not I pray you pollicy alwais ouermastered force? who subdued *Ha-*
nibal in his great royalty? he ý durst knock
at Rome gates to haue thē opened is nowe
become a pray to a sylly senator . *Appius*
Claudius et senex et cæcus a father full of
wisedome can releue the state of decaying
Rome. and was it force that subdued *Mari-*
us ? or armes that discouered *Catulins* con-
spiracies? was it rash reuendg in punishing
Cethegus ? or want of witt in the discourye
of treason? *Cato* can correct himselfe for tra-
ueling by Sea, when the land profereth pas-
sage, or to be sole hardy in ouer mutch ha-
zard. *Aristotle* accompteth counsell holpe, &
Socrates can terme it the key of certentye.
what shal we count of war but wrath, of bat-
tel but hastines, and if I did rule (with *Au-*
gustus Cæsar) I woulde refuse these coun-
selers. what made ý oracle I praye you accōpt of *Calchas* so much ? was it not for
his wisedome? who doth not like of the go-
uerner that had rather meete with *Vnum*
Nestorem then *decem Aiaces* ? you cannot
tame a Lyon but in tyme, neither a Tigres
in few dayes. Counsell in *Regulus* will pre-
ferring the liberty of his country before his
lyfe, not remit the deliuery of *Carthaginian*
captiues

captiues, Hanibal shall flesh himselfe on an
olde mans carkas, whose wisedome preser-
ued his citye. Adrian with letters can gouerne hys legions, and rule peasablye his
prouinces by policye. aske Siluius Italicus
what peace is and he will say?

Pax optima rerum quas homini nouiſſe.
　datum eſt, pax vna triumphis
Innumeris potior, pax custodire salutem.
　Et ciues æquare potens.

No better thing to man did nature
Euer giue then peace,
Then which to know no greater ioy,
Can come to our encrease.
To foster peace is stay of health,
And keepes the land in ease.

Take cousell of Ouid what sayth he?
Candida pax homines, trux decet atra feras.
Tó men doth heauenly peace pertaine,
And currish anger fitteth brutish vaine?

Well as I wish it to haue continuance, so
I praye God wyth the Prophet it be not a-
bused. and because I think my selfe to haue
sufficiently answered that I supposed, I
conclude

conclude wyth this. God preserue our peac-
able princes, & confound her enemies. God
enlarge her wisdom, that like *Saba* she may
seeke after a *Salomon*: God confounde the i-
maginations of her enemies, and perfit his
graces in her, that the daies of her rule may
be continued in the bonds of peace, that the
house of the chosen Israelites may be mayn-
teyned in happinesse: lastly I frendly
bid Gosson farwell, wyshinge
him to temper his penn
with more discre-
tion.

FINIS.